Chance Encounters and True Love

A Male's perspective

A
Collection of
Short Stories
Poems
and
Other Writings

I0566614

By
English L Jackson IV

Edited by
English L Jackson IV

About the Author

This is most likely the hardest part of the book to write. I have never liked talking about myself, but here it goes.

I was born in the great state of Texas, and returned after the Navy, to a very small town in Texas where I live now with my elderly father.

I am 45 years old at the time of writing these short stories and other ramblings. I am divorced, I am grateful for the experience and all the things that I learned about myself and the myriads of emotions that came along with being married and going through a divorce.

All these short stories in this book are fiction. Fiction is just another word for lie. But, with any great lie there is truth to be told to make it believable. Thus, I weave into these tales truth about myself.

I am retired from the US Navy. I severed twenty years. I have traveled around the world in a complete circle. I drew upon places that I visited and lived in trying to capture why I loved traveling which is the culture of all the places that I have been.

I am currently a college student. By the time this book hits the streets I should only have a year and a half to finish my Bachelor of Science degree in Biology. What do I plan on doing afterwards? I have entertained the idea of becoming a high school Biology teacher. I am also entertaining the idea of getting a second Bachelor of Science in Phycology, but I will see.

Some of you will want to know if I am going to continue to write? The answer is yes. I love writing it is part of who I am, and some weird way my own personal therapy. I do not want to get your hopes up by saying what I just said. I will write, but I'm not sure if I will publish again.

The female characters in these short stories are fictional. I did, however, base one character off a lovely young lady that I know. I will leave it at that. If she reads this book, she will know.

I am really a very simple guy, that had an idea and put it down on paper. I really do hope that you enjoy these short stories.

Table of Contents

Chance Encounter

Chapter One: The Meeting

We are sitting in a downtown coffee shop, it is close to closing time, and it is time for me to say fare well. We walked out into the hot humid summer night. A sheer lining of perspiration covers both of our bodies. I look at you and beauty transforms to exquisite loveliness in front of my very eyes.

You notice me looking at you and you know that I want you; you can see it, smell it, even taste it in the sweet sticky air. Your animal instincts are taking over. Your rational mind snaps back, 'But I just met him, I don't really know him, and I have a boyfriend.'

We continue to walk and make small talk getting to know each other a little better, with every given detail of our lives.

You hear a voice inside of you that is unfamiliar, You want him, he treats you like the lady that you are, he is a nice guy he does not deserve to finish last, at least not tonight.'

You look up at me and see that expression of desire and want. You know that I have not once acted upon these basic impulses, you think, 'He is a true gentleman.'

We are two blocks from where we parked. You reach down and take my hand and gently guide me away from the street into an unlit alley. Your touch, your first touch sends explosive waves of excitement coursing through my body.

You lead me far enough down the alley where no prying eyes would be able to see. You push me back against the wall and race your hands from my shoulders down my chest to my pants.

My thoughts are all over the place, I can't concentrate on any one thing, so I let the pleasure of your touch wash over me like a gentle warm wave lapping at the beach.

You have my cock in your hand slowly stroking it to life; you lick the tip, then the length of my shaft. As your other hand reaches under your dress and slowly starts to massage your clit.

My heart is pounding in my chest, my brain is dead at this point, I am working on pure instincts now.

You take my cock in your eager little mouth, your lips sliding up and down on my pulsing cock. You look up at me with your eyes that you must have stolen from an angel with a naughty side.

I feel like a child in a toy store and candy shop all in one, and I can have it all. That is exactly what I'm going to do is take it all.

My hands are keeping your hair out of your face that even a master sculpture could not replicate. I move my hands under your cheeks and gently lift you up.

Our eyes locked, an eternity passes by in a single instant, nothing else matters to the both of us. You feel my hard cock pressing against your flat stomach. I kiss you hard and deep. Your juices are flowing wanting me more now than you thought possible.

We trade places now your back is up against the wall we are still kissing. A hundred people could be watching but we are so lost to the outside world we would never notice.

I spin you around and reach under your dress and pull down your little white panties. You spread your legs inviting me in. I lean in my chest on your back; you can feel my heart pounding in my chest. You can feel the tip of my cock brushing up against your clit.

You start to sway your hips, which increases the pressure that my cock is applying on your clit. I lean in and whisper, "Are you sure you want to do this?" The only reasonable thought that I have had since we entered the alley. With a word, if one could call it that, it was more of a pleasure moan, but your answer was yes.

My cock penetrates your garden of pleasure, so tight, so wet. You whimper as my cock enters you for the first time. You turn your head so that you can see me, while I push my cock's full length in your wanting pussy.

You know you must be quiet, but you let out a seductive sigh, that drives me crazy. I begin to retract my cock as slow as I inserted it, more sighs of pleasure. I push myself back in this time a little faster than before.

You begin to gyrate your hips allowing my cock to reach all your hidden pleasure spots, that no one has ever found, until now. You cannot control yourself, the risqué of fucking in public, fucking a man that you barely know, even cheating on your boyfriend is all mind blowing and increasing the pleasure.

I can sense that you are about to cum and my thrusting becomes faster and harder with each in and out. Your body starts to quiver, your eyes start to roll up, your back arches, your head tilts back and you explode. I can feel you cumming all over my cock deep inside you.

You are trying to catch your breath as you push your hips against me, so my cock stays deep and nested in your tight wet pussy. You regain some control over your body and slowly pull away from my cock. You let out a tiny sigh when my cock fully exits you.

You turn to face me and bring me close to you no two bodies have ever been this close in the history of man-kind. You kiss me, and I kiss you back. You lift one leg, I help support you with one arm. You guide my cock back to your waiting pussy. We break all rules that are applied to sex, we don't close our eyes we stare deep into each other's eyes. It is like we can feel what the other is feeling compounding the pleasure ten-fold.

We kiss. We bite each other's lips. We bite on each other's necks. I pull down the strap of your dress to expose your bare breasts, nipples hard pointing towards me. I arch my back and take one nipple at a time and gently nibble on them. Your hands are holding and guiding me to which one you want to be played with all while I'm thrusting long hard strokes deep inside of you.

You have lost all control, and your moaning is louder you wish that someone was watching us. You wish that your boyfriend could see you now fucking a man you don't know, making you cum. With those thoughts you cum for the second time.

You don't press down on my cock this time you start to ride it the best way you can in this standing position, grinding on my cock every third stroke.

As your second climate ends the third begins this time your body freezes up you have no control, your leg I was holding up comes crashing down, your arms fly around my neck, your pussy tightens around my cock. I can't move in fear of hurting you. I wrap my arms around you, your entire body is shaking, you can barely speak.

Still standing there holding you, your body jumps uncontrollably with spikes of pleasure. You have never felt anything like this before. You realize that sex with any other man will never be the same.

You begin to relax, and tell me, "Fuck my little pussy!" With that I start thrusting again so close to cumming myself I ask, "where do you want it?"

I pull my cock out while you are sliding down to your knees. You put your lips around my cock sliding my cock deep into your mouth. You feel the first gush of my warm cum hit the back of your throat, you move up the shaft keeping the head of my cock in your mouth another burst and another. I can feel your tongue tickling the tip while you use your hand to stroke my cock and sucking all the cum from my cock.

You remove my cock with your hand looking at it so that you do not miss a drop of cum, when you are certain no more is to be had you begin to raise, your head down slightly but looking up with those eyes. I tell you to swallow it all. You give me a devilish grin, and you swallow, your lips part slightly as you lick your lips, then bite your lower lip and swallow again.

Chapter Two: The Departure

After we compose ourselves, we depart the alley like thieves in the night, ensuring no one sees us escaping. You are by my side holding my arm and resting your head on my shoulder as we walk the rest of the way to the parking lot.

You ask, "What time is it?" The coffee shop closed at ten o'clock, and then the alley, so it could not be that much past that I thought to myself.

I looked at my cell phone and it showed that it was eleven: thirty. I tell you and you're in a hurry to find your phone, almost panicking. I realize that you needed to be somewhere or call someone at a certain time and that time has had passed by a considerable amount. My heart sank into my stomach knowing that I was the cause of the mess that you are in right now.

You break away from me and put a little distance between us while dialing the person you needed to explain away your absence to. I could only assume it was your boyfriend that you were calling. I felt a pain in my chest knowing that I'm the reason that you are going to have to lie, not that you cheated.

Your call ends and you come back to my side as if nothing happened. "Is everything alright?" I asked.

"Nothing to worry about." You said

I'm dreading every step we take, closer to the ending of what is the greatest day of my life.

The universe has a funny way of playing with people. I backed up into my parking space, and you happened to park next to me, where both driver side doors were facing each other.

The end is upon us; time to walk away. I know I will see you again, in my dreams, fantasies, and when you perform on the cam-site, but never to touch, taste, smell or hear your moans of pleasure that I provided you ever again.

I reach down to kiss you good night one last taste of your sweet lips, you do not turn away. The kiss ends slowly. We both feel that this, whatever this is, should not end, not like this. You turn to open your car door; I wait until you are in before I get into my truck.

Once I'm inside I start the engine and feel the cool air cooling my soaked body. I rest my head on the steering wheel.

I hear a knock on my window; you are standing there. I roll down the window to make sure everything is alright.

You reach in and pull me into another long deep kiss. We are pulling each other to get closer but the door separates us. The kiss ends, and I say "Get in." You hurry to the other side, once you are in another passionate kiss begins. I can feel my cock spark back to life as you reach down between my legs.

I put my truck into drive and started heading out of the parking lot. You ask, "Where are we going?"

I answer, "Do you trust me?"

The answer did not come quick, but you did say, "Yes."

The drive seemed to last a lifetime, but you kept me distracted with one of your hands on my cock and your other rubbing your clit.

Once we arrived and you saw where we were, you kissed me again, and crawled on top of me, "Not here." I said.

Again, the night puts the sheer gleaming on our skin. You could hear it in the distance, a serenity of calmness, but with the power to destroy. You take my hand and hurriedly pull me towards the sound.

The gentle barely audible sound grew in volume with each step. Once we were in front of the thing making this peaceful music you stopped and stared out into its vastness.

Standing there under the stars and moon, in the sultry night, you say to me, "Thank you." You don't turn to me, afraid that I would see the tears forming in your eyes. I did not need to see them to know, I could hear them in your voice.

You were swimming in an ocean of emotions and thoughts as vast as the one before you. Calm, at peace, lust, love, passion, and fear; rational thoughts mixed with nonrational thoughts. Your world was changing and for the better or worse you could not tell, but in this moment, you knew, that this man, a one of a kind understood you.

You turn to me; you wipe the tears from your eyes and come closer to me. You embrace me. Placing your head on my chest. "I'm sorry, I'm crying." You say.

"Don't be, for whatever reason, you needed to let it out. I'm honored you were brave enough to do it in front of me." I say in a comforting voice.

You chuckle nervously, and look up at me with your amazing eyes, tears still there catching snips of light from the stars and moon to make them sparkle.

I kiss you again filled with pure passion.

I rent a hotel room, it is two in the morning, both of us are exhausted. "I'm going to take a shower." I tell you. While in the shower for no more than three minutes I feel your hands on my back. I turn and see all your majestic beauty before me, and you say, "I need a shower too."

Our bodies again take control, my cock springs to life, as your pussy starts to self-lubricate, wanting me inside you again.

Our bodies become a tangled mess in the shower, until you lose your balance, but I catch you before you fall, it is time for us to move out of the shower.

I take you by the hand and lead you to the bed. I spin you around once at the foot of the bed. I come in close you can feel my cock press up against you. I start to lean into you forcing you into a controlled slow fall back onto the bed.

You safely land on the bed; your knees are at the edge. I place my hands on them and pull them apart. You offer no resistance. Your breathing becomes sporadic, holding your breath between inhales and exhales.

The anticipation is driving you wild, you feel yourself becoming wetter and wetter.

10

I lean into your exposed pussy and in one motion lick. This first one of the night an unhindered sigh escapes from your lips. Lips that you are biting.

My tongue dances to the perfect beat around your clit, bringing you to cum within seconds. Your legs squeeze together pinning my head and tongue snug against your wet pussy.

I put my hands under your perfect ass, and lift bringing your pussy closer to me. My tongue parts your lips and I taste your sweet nectar.

You feel my tongue enter you, you begin to rock your hips up and down cradled in my hands. You wish this would never stop, but you want my cock deep inside you again.

I continue my tongue torture until you cum a second time. Your juices flow, and I drink it up like a man dying of thirst.

I release my hold on your ass, and let it fall back to the bed, you laugh with the sudden change, you enjoy it, you want more.

You position yourself fully on the bed now, and I crawl slowly, kissing your body all the way up to your lips. You can taste yourself on my lips.

You reach down and take hold of my cock, you use it to rub your clit, having the tip spread your lips, teasing the entrance to your pussy, even circling your tight little asshole.

You raise your hips to a position yourself for my cock to be inserted into that very tight ass. You guide the tip to the spot, and I start to push my way inside, slowly.

You gasp as the head fully enter your ass and begin to breathe rapidly as the full length is inserted. I slowly retract, and you start rocking your hips again, this creates micro thrusting, while I'm pulling out of you.

I start the second thrust inwards, and you say, "Faster!" I push a little faster, again you say, "Faster!" Again, I obey. "Fuck my ass!" With that last command, I thrust the full length into your willing ass, and slide out just as fast, and slam it back in, a slapping sound is heard from our bodies colliding together. This is not gentle, this is rough anal sex now.

You say, "Don't stop; don't stop! Harder, harder!"

I'm fucking your ass with all that I have, and your body freezes your ass clamps down on my cock so fiercely that I cannot move. Your body is paralyzed with pleasure. Your arms are stiff, your hands have a death grip on the sheets, your head is arched back.

You forget who you are, where you are, this new-found drug that is coursing through your body would make a fortune if there was a way to sell it. You are instantly addicted, wanting more, needing more, and the only way to get more is to continue letting me fuck you.

Your body begins to shake with pleasure, and you stammer, "More, please give me more." You have never pleaded for anything in your life before, but you can't help yourself now.

I exit your tight little ass. "No don't stop!" You beg of me. I position myself and insert my cock into your unexpecting pussy. You melt, a total loss of control.

Your head rolls to the side, you are breathing heavily through your parted lips.

When I am fully inside you, I lean in to kiss you, you try to kiss me back, but you can't, this drug is not allowing you to.

I realize what is happening, so I stop, I exit you and you whimper as I leave. A minute or two goes by, as I lay next to you. You start to regain control and say, "I'm sorry, I don't know what happened."

I reply, "Nothing to be sorry about."

The hunger starts to grow inside you again, giving you a second wind, you roll me over onto my back, and you straddle me. You place my cock back inside your wet pussy. You are in control of everything now.

You let your hips raise and fall on my cock, wanting and needing that feeling again. You lean back you take my ankles in your hands as you continue to ride me. I begin to rub your clit with one of my thumbs, your moans become louder, and louder.

Your body starts to shake, you have found the place where this drug hides, you are just in reach of it. You tell yourself, "One more dose, then I will stop."

You lean forward and start kissing me while only moving your hips up and down in quick secession. You can see the drug in your mind's eye you are so close.

Your hips move even faster; you are at arm's length from the drug. Your moaning has become even louder, you are telling me to, "Fuck me harder!"

The drug is in your hand, a small vial of crystal-clear liquid, with a cork stopper. You pry the stopper out a sweet scent escapes, you place the vial to your lips and stop.

I grab your hips holding them motionless as I thrust my cock in you. You look at me panting and say "I want you to fill my pussy with your cum. Cum inside me!"

With that I drop my hold of your hips you drop down on my cock, you feel it deep inside you. We find each other's pace and fuck as hard as we can.

You feel the first shot of warm cum deep inside your wet pussy. You flash to the vial at your lips, and greedy drink it all. The second explosion of cum deep inside your wanting pussy. Large exhales escape you. You feel the effects of this drug again, this time stronger than before. A third eruption of cum in your hungry pussy. You are gone again. Pure peace, every inch of your body is on fire, tingling with sensations that you have never felt before.

You fall on top of me, breathing hard, and not moving, while I am still inside of you.

I feel you start to tremble. I wrap my arms around your perfect body; I kiss your neck gently. You move slowly to brush your hair to the side, so my kisses are unhindered.

You look at me, I can see that your eyes are still puffy from crying. My heart melts at the sight. I understand what just happened. You may never admit it, or claim that it happened, but I saw it with my own two eyes.

I try to position myself so that I can better hold you. You stop me, and say, "I want you inside me a little longer." I reach up and kiss you.

CHICAGO

Because of my Naval career I was able to visit, see and experience many places around the world that most would only dream about seeing. The place it all started though was a place that I did not get to experience.

I am walking down a street in Chicago, taking it all in, it is ten in the morning already hot and humid, but nothing that I am not used to.

I pass a little bar the red neon 'Open' sign draws me in. 'Why not, I have not had a beer or two in a while', I think to myself.

I walk in and like every bar the lights are dim, a row of booths line one wall, the opposite wall is where the bar sits, a few round tables and chairs here and there. There is no real theme to the bar, it is not a sports bar or a biker bar just a neighborhood bar.

While walking to the bar I see that two men are sitting at one of the round tables talking and drinking a couple of beers, and another sitting at the bar with his back to the front door.

I take a seat furthest from the front door at the bar. I pull out a twenty and place it on the tabletop.

From where I am sitting I cannot see you, you are crouched under the bar doing some type of maintenance or cleaning. A couple of seconds go by and you pop up, your back is to me.

Nice figure, great timing for wanting a beer.

You look around the bar and you see me sitting at the end of the bar and walk over to me. "Sorry about the wait, what can I get you?" You asked, while looking down at your hands while drying them on your bar towel.

"I would like a beer, from a bottle, but poured in a mug if you have one, if it is not too much trouble." I asked.

You look up as you hear me speak, my accent gave it away that I am not from this area, or state.

I see your true beauty looking at me. You smile and turn to make my order. You bend straight legged to reach down into the cooler. Your black skirt raises up a little, showing off more of your prefect legs. I know why you did this, a female bartending trick, flirt a little, makes for larger tips, and I was certain you always made your fair share of the tips. The same trick could not be done to get the mug from the freezer though.

You walk over and pour the beer in front of me, "That will be $4.00 sweetie." You let me know.

I pick the twenty up and hand it to you. You come back with the change. "I will be back in two seconds." You tell me.

"That's prefect since it will take at least three for me to drink this." I reply. You give a little laugh.

When you return you wipe the bar in front of me then rest your forearms on the clean area. "So, you are not from here judging by your accent." You pause, "The south, but not the east coast south."

I nod in agreement, making it harder now for you without hearing the accent again.

"I'm going to say Alabama.?" A question more than a statement or guess.

I smile and do what I think would be an Alabama accent, "I do hate to inform you pretty lady; that I am in fact not from ALLAA-BAAMMM-AAAAH."

You laugh, "That was amazing, and true you don't sound like that." The most beautiful smile I have ever seen appears in front of me.

"I just can't place it." Giving up or trying to move the conversation on, you say.

"I'm from a place where Ya'll, over yonder, fixin' to, and every soda is a coke, is used daily." I say.

You are still unsure, I say, "I will use those words in a real everyday conversation." I put the accent a little heavy as I speak, "I'm fixin' to head over yonder, ya'll want a coke or sumthin?"

You laugh out loud. "I have no idea what you just said, but it..." You stopped not to offend me or where I call home.

"I am from Texas." I let you know.

"You don't have that type of accent, southern, but would have never guessed." You smile a genuine smile.

You think to yourself this man is funny, seems intelligent, but poor taste in beer, but we all have our flaws as you walk away, holding up one finger, you are at work you do have duties to take care of.

When you return you ask, "What brings you to the Windy City?"

I say, "Just here to see the sites, and live the experience that I missed the first time I was here." I shake my head side to side. "Where are my southern manners?" with that I introduce myself. You tell me your name, and we shake hands.

"I see, reliving your past? What does your present self, do?" You ask.

"I am a college student." I reply to the second question.

"That's great." You say with a smile on your face and continue with, "I was in a high-end science field degree plan and halfway through I changed it and finish in the Arts field of study."

I set my drink down, I smile and say, "That is amazing."

You looked shocked; I could tell that most people that you tell this to do not agree with my statement, then you said with what seemed like a voice filled with defeat, "Yeah amazingly dumb."

I reached out to touch your arm resting on the bar and said, "No, truly amazing, you followed your heart, your passion. Damn those who believe what is, and what is not considered an intelligent field of study. That surgeon sure may be intelligent in some things but not all. Take a musician that makes it big, his or her song touches more lives the first time it is played than that surgeon could ever save in a lifetime. The painter that inspires some math genius a hundred years from now. The writer that carries their reader to a new place, or new time. These people who create art, to me are the most intelligent people, they use a finite medium to capture a feeling, a thought, a moment in space and time and share it with the world for pure betterment. No other profession can claim such brilliance."

You are caught on every word, this man that you just met, understands you more than any other person in your life. You think of your boyfriend, a good man, he loves you, you love him but have never connected like this. A missing puzzle piece just fell into place. You feel a tingle race down your spine, it explodes at the small of your back. You realize and think to yourself, 'Why am I getting wet?'

I pull my hand from your arm; you reach and take my hand. "Thank you, you have made my day, hell my year." You excuse yourself and walk to the back where the store room is located.

You wipe the forming tears from your eyes; you take a deep breath. The feeling between your legs is becoming stronger. You reach down and start to rub yourself; you stop before you cannot stop, knowing that customers are out in the bar.

You come back and bend over the cooler once again, I look up. Your skirt is hiked a little higher this time I can see the bottom of you perfect round ass, where it meets your beautiful legs. You shift your weight from one leg to the other you skirt slides up a little higher. I can see your black panties hugging your ass cheeks. You stand up straight, you adjust your skirt back down to normal wear.

You come back to where I was sitting. The two customers sitting together get up and wave their good-byes. You thank them and say, "See you tomorrow." You take my empty mug and replace it with a fresh one, open a new beer and start to pour. "This one is from me."

If I had a hat on, I surely would have tipped it towards you, but I said, "Where I come from, normally if a bartender buys a drink for someone, that someone buys the bartender a drink."

"I can't." You say.

"I insist, anything you want." I rebuttal.

"I like where you are from." You say with a smile.

You turn and pull a shot glass from the shelf, then a bottle of tequila you pour the shot to the rim. You come back, with grace at which your body moved, allowed not a single drop to leave the tiny glass.

You hold up your drink and say, "To all the intelligent people of the world."

I raise my glass and say, "I can drink to that." We tap the glasses together; you finish yours with a single head tilt. I, myself cannot, but I do finish half of my beer.

Small talk continues leading into more personal details. The flirting continues, light touching at first, turns to petting of the back side of your hand.

My touch is wrong, but you allow it. The touch of my fingertips on your soft skin sends warning signs to your mind. 'STOP! STOP!' But something else, something basic, something void of all rational thoughts is taking over. You want me.

You pull away and say to the other customer sitting at the other end of the bar, by name, "Time to go, need to do some cleaning before the big rush." He does not say anything but slowly gets up and walks to the door.

I, myself start to stand, and take the last of my beer down. You wave towards me to get my attention, and motion me to sit back down.

You follow the man out, you look both ways down the street, you lock the door, and flip off the neon sign that invited me in.

You do not say a word, you walk behind the bar, grab the bottle of tequila, another beer and walk around the bar. You sit next to me.

"What is your custom for when a bartender closes a bar for someone?" You ask with lust in your voice.

I turn to better face your beauty to see all of you, sitting there wanting me to take you. I reach up and cup my hand at the nape of your neck, I pull you in to kiss you.

You do not stop me and once again all the warnings are telling you to stop, but you kiss me back. My other hand finds itself on your leg softly kneading it with tender pressure.

You break away from the kiss and you turn your head to the side. Your exposed neck is there to be kissed from a hungry vampire, I attack kissing, gently biting, pulling your skin gently with my lips. While my other hand makes it way closer and closer to your garden.

You feel my kisses on your neck, my fingertips lightly on the inside of your thigh. Your mind is moving too quickly to stay on one thought. The only thing that you can think about or truer to the sense is the feeling of pleasure.

My hand arrives at your secret garden I can feel the contours of what lays beneath. I slowly start to massage your wanting pussy.

A sigh escapes your beautiful lips you spread your legs ever so slightly allowing my hand, and fingers easier access.

You cannot believe you are doing this at your place of work, with a customer, a perfect stranger. A rush of excitement of all these things releases a wave of small trimmers through your body. You just came with a single touch, you want more, you want me, you must have me now.

You reach down and start rubbing my crouch, you unbutton my pants and slide the zipper down. You put your hand down my pants. You take hold of my cock and slowly begin to stroke up and down.

My hand that was on the back of your neck moves to your shoulders, moving your shirt and bra strap away and down your arm. My lips follow kissing your shoulder then your exposed collar bone. I continue to pull your shirt until your perfectly sculptured breast appears.

The cool air from the air conditioning reaches your expose nipple instantly it becomes hard. My tongue makes small circles around it.

You think every day should be like this. Tingling goose bumps race across your skin.

I take your nipple in my mouth. I gently apply pressure on it with my lips and roll it with the side-to-side motion while the tip of my tongue dances on the tip of your nipple.

My hand moves to the edge of your panties and pull them to the side, allowing my fingers full range of your garden. My hand slides up just enough that my middle fingertip rest on your clit. With slight pressure and a circling motion start my work in this magical garden of yours.

You sigh at the touch, breathing faster and faster keeping pace with my finger rubbing your clit. You cannot take much more. You stand up and take my hand and lead me back to the storeroom.

Once there I turn you to face me and kiss your inviting lips. You kiss me back. Our hands are all over each other. Nothing can stop this, you know it and want it to happen, and I know it and want it to happen.

I turn you to face the wall and I lift your skirt. You look back at me, your eyes are telling me you want to feel me inside of you. I pull your black panties down. You reach down between your legs and start to massage your already wet pussy, as if telling it to get ready it answered with lubing itself even more.

My pants are down, and my cock is toying with your pussy. This is maddening to you, in a good way, the tease, the anticipation. I enter your lovely garden without warning. Your eyes roll your head tilts back, you feel the full length of me inside you. The shock makes you retract your hips a split second, then you push back you feel me deep inside you.

'What are you doing?' You think. The same thoughts as before, but how can this be wrong. Everyone should feel this good.

You continue to rock your hips as I thrust inside of you. Pleasure moans and sighs leave your parted lips. With each thrust you feel as if you are walking towards a cliff edge, a crashing surf below waiting for you. Feelings of fear and excitement tangle into a new unnamed feeling. You want to run and throw yourself off this cliff and be damned what waits below, damn the warnings, you are here, and there is no place left to go. You do not run you place one foot in front of you, you feel me enter you; the other foot in front of the last, you feel me retract. Step after step, closer and closer to the edge.

I spread your ass with my hands, I spit. With one hand I use a finger to rub it around your tight little asshole. You do not resist.

You find yourself at the very edge; you turn around and you can see everything in your life that led up to this moment. The craziness of your life, and if one thing was different, this chance encounter would never have happened. You know at this point with all the good and bad, you would not change a thing to miss out on this.

You lean back allowing gravity to take hold; I insert my thumb into your tight ass. Weightlessness, time stands still, the truest meaning of peace and calmness fills you.

Your body shakes when the first shot erupts deep inside you. You feel my cum, warm and deep inside you; you want more, as you, yourself cum on my cock inside you.

Your descent is slow yet powerful, you feel the wind around your body, you know that this unnamed feeling will not let any harm come to you. You feel safe as the wind passes around you.

A second thrust and a push from your hips sends another shot deep inside you.

You feel the mist from the waves below. A cool sensation on your warm skin sends uncontrollable shivers through your body, you inhale deeply knowing you will be in the grasp of the tide very soon.

I push myself as deep as I can, another eruption. You whimper, your body shakes, you are getting weak.

You are now in the arms of the waves, caressing your body with gentle warm touches. Your body and mind are completely relaxed. You have had great partners in the past, even my blowing orgasms. This, whatever this is; nothing can compare to it. You know this was not making love, love has no part in this, but it was not just sex or two people fucking. It came to you in a flash like a lightning bolt and with the same power that it carries through the sky. We made Art.

I catch your falling body. I slowly help you regain your balance. You look up at me, this man you just met a few hours ago, that with the soft-spoken words of kindness, could have an effect over you, not just the pleasure of the flesh, but in your thoughts that would change your outlook on life.

You kiss me deeply, you want me again, but the bar must be re-opened.

We straighten up ourselves and walk back to where the beer you brought me had condensation all over the bottle. You unlock the door. You walk back over to me and kiss me again. You get me a fresh beer.

"I will be right back, need to freshen up." As you head to the ladies room.

A man enters the bar, nods towards me as a greeting and looks around. He then asks where you might be.

I let him know that you just went to the ladies room. He nods and takes a seat at the middle of the bar.

You walk out; your body language changes. "Sweetie, how are you? Good day at work?" As you look at your phone checking the time. You think where did the time go?

He smiles truly happy to see you, "Better now that I can see you."

I sat quietly drinking my beer. Loosing myself in my thoughts of what just happened and happening now. The what ifs of the world start creeping in.

You come back over to me and say, "Still want a shot?" Covering for why the bottle and shot glass were on the bar next to where I was sitting.

"No thank you. I should be going."

Your boyfriend interrupts and says, "Nonsense, I owe you a beer. She told me what you said about the intelligence thing and how it made her day, for that I owe you at least a beer."

I wanted to laugh out loud, the universe works in crazy ways, and if he only knew everything, he would not want to buy me a beer but use one to beat me with.

"Sure, one more will not hurt." I say to him and then look at you.

England

Chapter One: Day One Lost

I am totally lost in this little town.

I decided to take my summer break from college and see some more of this beautiful crazy world that we all live in. I am not the typical college student. I have retired from the US Navy. I stay home and take care of my elderly father, so I do not have a job per say, my retirement is enough for now.

I am twice the age of most of the other students; most men my age, go out and buy a new sports car, I go back to school. My time is spent at school or studying and taking care of my Dad. I am not drawn into the drama that the other students seem to strive for. I do not worry myself if she or he likes this or that person, nor do I care where the next big party is. I did that, been there, now it is time for school, might be the reason that my grades are at the top of each of my classes, it is not that I am smarter than anyone else.

I continue walking down this street and up ahead of me, I see a little coffee shop. I am going to have to swallow my pride and ask for directions. I notice a lady sitting with her back to me. Shoulder length hair gently dancing in the cool summer breeze. I think to myself without even seeing all of her, 'She has to be a beauty.'

I walk inside the quite shop. I look through the window to where you are sitting outside. I stop in my tracks. My eyes must be playing a trick on me or still

27

tired from the jet lag. Sitting just on the other side of this window is an angel.

"May I help you?" asked the lady behind the counter. This broke off my rude stare. My mind was lost in thought just as I am lost in this town. I had forgotten the reason why I walked in. I did not know what type of shop this was. The smell of delicious coffee reminded me where I was.

"Yes, I would like a cup of coffee to go please." I said, stealing glances over my shoulder to ensure my eyes were not playing tricks on me.

"You are an American, what brings you to this part of England?" She asks.

"The sites." I reply not looking away from you.

"Not too many of those around here." She continues.

"I see one." I say not meaning to say it out loud.

"Pardon me?" She asks.

"Oh! Nothing, it is that there is one I want to see." I do my best to cover up the slip that just escaped my lips.

I paid for the coffee, thanked her and watched you through the window as I walked to the door. You did not notice that I was looking at you while I was in the shop.

I walked up behind you I gently place my hand on your shoulder and said, "Excuse me Miss."

You give a little jump and gasp as the shock and surprise of my touch on you shoulder.

You turn to look at whoever just interrupted your thoughts. You see that I have taken a step back and holding my hands up in front of my chest as a gesture of I am sorry, surrender, and I come in peace. I say, "I am so sorry that I startled you, please forgive me."

The shock wears off; you let out a tiny little giggle of nerves. It is music to my ears. "It is fine. You are an American?" You say, in a soft voice that only angels can possess.

"I get that a lot around here, I guess it is my accent or the way I butcher proper English." I say with a smile.

Another sound of music reaches my ears you giggle at what I just said. My mind forgot what I wanted to do today. All I wanted now was to get to know this lovely creature, this perfect being sitting in front of me.

You ask, "Is there something you wanted?"

My mind races looking for the answer, an answer that would allow me to get to know you better.

"Oh! Yes, I hate to admit this, but I am lost." I let the defeat sound in my voice. Then I tell you everything that happened up to this point, I told you the truth. Then I say, "You must here it all the time, but you are beautiful."

With that and knowing what is to come I say in my best British accent, "I will take my leave, my good lady." I turned and started to walk away.

A true laughter escapes, I with my back to you I start to walk away, I smile. You reach for my hand, you touch it, causing me to stop. I turned around. You tried to hide it, but I saw that you were biting your lower lip ever so lightly. On any other day you would have let me walk away, or told me to get lost, maybe it was because I was lost already and that is why you did what you did.

You ask me to sit, "Finish your coffee with me, then I will tell you were to find what you are looking for."

I could not come out and say it, but you were what I was looking for. We introduce ourselves and start with the basics of two people getting to know each other. But, not as mundane as what is your favorite color. I even spell it differently.

My cup of coffee is almost empty, and I do not want this exchange to end so I ask, "Would you like another cup?" You smile and say, "That would be lovely." You let me know what you like, and I head back inside for the second time.

"Find what you were looking for?" The lady behind the counter asks, remembering the first time I walked in.

I say, "I do believe that I have." With a smile on my face.

I return with the coffees I set yours down in front of you; you thank me. Then you ask, "Tell me what in this town does a traveling American want to see?" You pick up your coffee with both hands holding it with just your fingertips. Slowly tilting the cup towards your luscious lips.

I try my best to explain in all the places that I have been, yes, the museums, the art that I have seen, the great architectural buildings that have stood the test of time. These things put a draw on people wanting to see them, so people travel and see things like that for themselves. But, for me it is not just these things that draw me in, it is the people, the culture that surrounds them. I find that pure beauty. Yes, the people may be gone that created these things, and cultures do shift, but the core of it remains and that is why I travel, to try and live it, be part of it, even if it is just for a moment.

You understand what I am saying. I then say to you, "So, if I am trying to see anything really at all, then I have seen part of it today."

You ask, "And what part have you seen today?"

I smile, and say, "I am looking at it right now. You have given me more than some priceless piece of art hanging on some wall, would ever give me, and for that I truly thank you."

You start to blush, the rose color feels your cheeks, you can feel the warmth rushing upwards. Your heart melts, this stranger that you just met, this American just touched a part of you that you had no idea that was inside of you. Your mind goes to a place of desire, you feel that your body is reacting to this desire, you can feel yourself becoming wet.

You shift your weight in your seat; you exhale a little longer than normal. No one could tell what is happening to you, not even myself, and I was sitting across this little round table from you.

Your rational mind takes over and starts asking questions. 'How are words doing this to me? Do you think he is attractive, or is it that he is a stranger, or possibly an American? Could it be all of these things?'

Our second cup of coffee is now finished, and I say "I should let you get back to enjoying your day. I have taken up too much of your time. It was an honor and pleasure of having met you; someone that is as lovely as you. Thank you again, you made this trip priceless."

I stand and take both empty cups to the trash. I turn and wave and start to walk away.

You sit there not wanting whatever this is to end. You want more, but what is it that you want. You look back and see me walking away. You are afraid, excited, if you are going to act you must do it now.

You stand, you take a deep breath and you follow after me. You call out my name asking me to wait. I stop and turn and see you walking towards me. It is not a walk, it is a graceful dance, a perfect dance keeping beat with my heart inside my chest.

You look at me and say, "What kind of representative of England would I be if I do not show you more of our culture." You giggle again. Which brings a smile to my face.

I ask, "Are you hungry, and do you know of any good places to eat?"

You take me to a little quite place where we eat and have a glass of wine, a truly lovely meal. Never in my wildest dreams would I have thought that traveling would have such a perfect day, sitting down with a Goddess and sharing a wonderful meal and time together.

I know that I am about to ruin all that has transpired up to this point, but I had to ask, "Forgive me if I am prying, but what about your boyfriend?"

You look up and say, "Are you serious? These blokes around here. They do not know how to treat a lady, they only think of themselves."

"I am sorry that I assumed but just look at you. An angel sent to live amongst us mere mortals not even deserving your glance in our direction. I would do anything in my power just to see you smile." I tell you.

With that you smile at my kind words. A thought flashes in your mind, you want me. You shake your head, trying to clear your thoughts.

I ask, "Everything alright?"

You take a drink, "A little too much salt on that last bite." Your mind races back to that thought. You picture what my cock may look like, you want it, you feel yourself getting wet again. A naughty side of you is trying to take over. You like this feeling; you want it to continue.

We finish our meal; I stand and offer my hand to help you out of your seat. You look at it, then back at me. I can see that no one has treated you like the lady you deserve to be treated like. You take my hand; you stand we walk out of the little restaurant.

We walk down this street and that street talking, laughing when you stop and look up. You let out a little nervous giggle. "This is my place." You say with a little surprise in your voice, that it was placed there as a ruse. You secretly lead us here, the naughty side taking complete control over you.

"It is getting late, and I should be getting back..."

You stop me by asking, "Would you like to come up and have a drink?"

My heart is now ponding in my chest. This must be a dream. I know any second that I will wake up and push my head out of a textbook that I am studying for an upcoming exam. The waking moment never arrived.

"Yes, I would love to." I answer. You take my hand and lead me inside.

Once inside you pour two glasses of wine. "Please sit." You say as you hand me the glass. I wondered if this is how Adam felt when Eve offered him the forbidden fruit. The temptation of lust, desire, pure animal instinct running rampant through their bodies, losing all control.

You sit close to me I take a sip; I can only image that your lips taste sweet. I set the glass down and look at you, our eyes lock, we kiss. You break away and set your glass down. You struggle to remove your shirt; my hands are there to help. Your breasts, perfect in every way, are hidden from view by your black lacy bra.

I kiss you; you start to pull my shirt up. My chest is exposed. You rub your hands up and down my chest. I reach behind you and unclasp your bra. I slide my hands up to your shoulders and slide the straps off. You remove your arms from the bra and toss it to the side.

We are hungry for each other; each kiss, each touch cannot satisfy this hunger it only makes it stronger. You reach down and start undoing my pants. My hands holding your head to the side while I kiss your silky neck.

The anticipation of what is to come is maddening you want me inside you, you can feel yourself becoming ready for my cock.

Our shoes have been kicked off; my pants are now off. I start working on yours. You pull your pants off lace black panties cover your wet wanting secrets.

You push me down on the couch. You remove my underwear and toss them to the side. You now see my cock you want it more than before. You lean down and lick the tip of it. A small uncontrollable jump of my cock from your tongue licking it causes you to do a naughty giggle, then you smile. It is like you have a new toy and you get to use it for the first time.

I reach up and take your hair; brushing it with my fingers to the back and hold it there in a make-shift ponytail. My other hand is placed on the side of your neck and slowly slides to your shoulder and down your arm.

You look up at me, I look down at you. A spark ignites and if left to its own it will... No one knows what will happen.

You feel my hand pulling you down. You let my cock part your sweet lips. The warmth of your mouth feels like being home from the cold brutal outside world.

You swirl your tongue around my cock as you move up and down the shaft. You reach up with one hand and lightly rake your fingernails down my chest, down to the base of my cock.

With your other hand you reach down and start massaging your secret spot over your panties.

You quickly raise up, my hand still holding your hair causes your head to turn to the side before I could release my grip. You did not seem to mind the slight pain of the accidental hair pulling. You slide your hands on either side of your perfectly shaped hips. You catch the thin straps of your panties in the crooks of your thumbs. You slowly start to push them down.

I lay there looking first in your eyes. I see you smile a devilish smile. You look down with only your eyes, telling me in an unspoken language to do the same. My eyes slowly move down your body following every line every curve that makes your body a true work of art. My eyes find what you wanted them to see.

Slowly more and more of your pubic area is shown, smooth, soft skin, fully shaven. Your secret is now in my sight. I want to be inside you more than ever.

You can see on my face that I am enjoying this show that you are doing for me. You feel sexy, naughty, you feel wrong, but you cannot stop. You do not pick up strangers and bring them back to your place type of wrong. 'But there is something about me.' You think to yourself.

Your panties are halfway down your lovely thighs and you lift and remove them and toss them to the pile of clothes forming on the floor. I reach out and take hold of your small waist and pull you on top of me.

Your hands catch yourself by bracing them on my chest, then you slowly lower the rest of the way down. I kiss you again.

I feel your soft breasts pressing against my chest. You can feel my hard cock pressing against your flat stomach.

You slide down your hand and start stroking my cock.

The spark was left unattended; it snaps and pops, no longer a spark, a tiny flame forms where it lands. You stand there watching this flame dance, a dangerous forbidden dance as it draws you closer.

36

You take my cock and slowly rub it around your wet secret. You do not want it to be a secret from me any longer. The tip of my cock slowly enters. Your secret, parts its lips to tell its tale.

When I enter you, a warmth of pleasure rushes through your body.

You see that the flame has grown, not a single flame like that of a candle, but not large enough to cause alarm. But the draw to it is stronger. You uncontrollably reach for it despite knowing what will happen. The flame jumps and licks your fingers as I enter you. On pure instincts you pull away and jump back from the flame. You realize there was no pain, warmth yes, but no pain. Where there should have been pain it is replaced with pleasure. You let yourself be drawn in again by the flame.

You slowly glide down on my cock, feeling as it fills you. Your breathing is slow; you are savoring each and every moment. I am fully inside you. You close your eyes and stay there only a second.

The flame has yet grown again to the size of that of a small campfire. You cannot take your eyes off it. You swear you see tiny figures dancing within the flames. You can feel the warmth on your naked body, so inviting, you want to dance with them, you want to be part of this desire.

You lift your hips and let them fall again. Your secret is telling me everything. You rock your hips forward and lift, then back down. You rock your hips back you lift, then back down.

You moan, your head tilts back, your back arches, your breast are pushed forward. I reach up and caress them. You do not know if you can take much more, but you continue you are determined to go as far as you can.

You reach into the fire with both hands, no pain. You see the tiny figures dancing on your hands. You lift them out of the flames they continue to dance their dance of desire in your palms. You slowly turn your hands over; these figures gracefully follow the turning of your hands and now dance on the backs of them. These tiny figures leave untraceable footprints but with each step they send waves of warmth throughout your body.

You fall on top of me, breathing in deeply and letting it out slowly. Your secret story has been told as you reached your first orgasm.

You turn your angelic face towards mine. You kiss me. Your skin is warm on my body. I slowly retract half of my length, and slide back in. You do not resist. You want more.

I slowly roll you over; I am on top of you. You lightly bite your lower lip. I lean down to kiss you. You wrap your legs around me to pull me closer to you. You reach up and pull my upper body down to lightly rest against yours.

This fire in your mind has spread throughout your body and has grown in size. No longer the small campfire but now a bonfire. You are further away from it than the tiny flame, or the campfire, but the warmth from it is stronger. You can see dancing figures circling it with their alluring movements.

I slowly enter you; you take a step closer to the bonfire. I retract; you take another step closer.

With each slow and gentle thrust you move closer to this bonfire. It seems to be growing in size, the warmth from the bonfire is warmer than the campfire, and still no pain, only pleasure. The dancing figures beckon you to join them.

You are afraid that you will lose yourself, but excited at the same time.

The first traces of perspiration appear between your prefect breasts. Our bodies touching every possible inch of skin that can be touched.

Your breathing has increased in speed, quick inhales, and faster exhales of moans and sighs.

These figures take your hands then embrace you. You feel the warmth of the embrace, you know after this embrace there will be no more, there cannot be more. The figure moves in closer and envelopes you completely.

You cum; cum on my cock deep inside you. Your legs squeeze tightly around me, pinning me inside. Your fingernails rake down my back.

A light sheer of perspiration covers your beautiful body giving it a glow that even angels would envy.

You are panting, trying to regain control. You have a conflict raging inside of you. Your mind is telling you to stop while your body is telling you that you want more. A stalemate of will of the mind verses strength of the body neither side is giving ground. An outside source tips the scales, and the body overcomes the mind.

I pull myself out of you. You open your eyes and look at me. You release your hold of me. I sit up and reach my hand to help you do the same. You take my hand but continue to raise up. You stand, and you lead me to your bedroom.

Once inside your room, you crawl on top of your bed. I felt the temperature jump in your room by ten degrees. Beauty, sex appeal and desire all radiate from you like heat waves on a hot summer's day.

I climb into your bed and position myself behind you.

I take my cock with a steady motion, and gently slide myself all the way in.

You could barely hear your own sounds of pleasure over the raging forest fire that now lies before you. Once again, it is warmer with no pain. There is something different this time there are no dancing figures. You have a slight hesitation, and realize it is all your choice now, nothing to draw you in but your own desire, your own want, your own need. You look behind you, there you can see where this all started, the tiny little flame, the campfire, the bonfire with the dancing figures. You take a step towards the bonfire and away from the forest fire that now blazes at your back. With that step, your body shivered. A coolness filled your body. You stop and take a step backwards the warmth returns.

You match my thrusts with the rocking of your hips. Your body shakes all over for a moment, then back to a relaxed state. You lower your head to the bed and continue to push yourself towards my cock.

You are at the invisible wall of flames. A revolutionary thought appears in your mind, turn back now.' You reach your hand into the wall. No more thoughts, only pleasure, true pure pleasure. A raw pleasure, a letting go, of all that is known, all that is true, at this point anything and everything is possible.

You step into the blaze, as my cock unloads the first shot of cum deep inside you.

With no pain you feel your body slowly melting away.

Your body relaxes your hips drop slightly, I thrust at the same time as your hips drop a longer thrust and deeper the second shot of cum inside you.

Only your thoughts remain. Everything is clear. All is known. For the first time in your life, you are free from everything, the social bonds and restrictions gone. You have found Utopia, Heaven, Zion, all these places rolled up into one.

Your hips fall to the bed again I thrust at the same time and gravity keeps me inside you. Your body hits the bed, my body crashes on top of you and erupts another round of cum inside you.

Your body has been reborn from the flames like the great Phoenix of myths and legends. A rebirth not just of the body but that of the mind as well.

You lay there still, breathing heavily. I move next to you. I gently touch the small of your back. You give a small jump, as if you have just been touched for the very first time. You turn your head to look at me, with what feels like to you, new eyes. You smile at me and lean in and kiss me.

41

You roll over; your back to my chest I wrap my arms around you to hold you. You feel safe, a serenity falls over you like a warm blanket. You close your eyes and fall asleep in the arms of a stranger.

Chapter Two: Day Two Hotel

I am at the waking point from a very deep sleep. My mind clearing the cobwebs, readying itself for the day. England; you; last night; my eyes pop open, you perfect body still laying there where you closed your eyes. My arms still wrapped around you.

You are holding one of my arms, as if even while sleeping you still wanted to touch me, feel me.

I gently pull my arm free, and as quietly as I can I get out of your bed. I find my clothes and I put on my pants. I pick up the two wine glasses still full from the night before and walk into the kitchen.

I could have eaten everything in sight. I normally skip breakfast and only have coffee but today I had to have something to eat. I put the two wine glasses in the sink. Then I started searching for food.

I open the small ice box and take stock of what you have and make a plan. I start working.

I return to your bedroom with a tray in hand. I pray a small little prayer to all the Gods, past, present, future and the unknowns to make sure that I get this right, that what I have prepared is to your liking.

I set the tray on the nightstand next to the bed, you have rolled over, most likely do the shift in weight in the bed after I left.

I sit on the edge of the bed; you stir just a bit. You are covered only by the sheet. The outlines of your body come through. I think, 'Such beauty, such peace.'

I lean down and gently kiss your cheek. You stir again and move your hand up to my cheek. I see that the kiss brings a smile to your already perfect face.

"Good morning, beautiful." I say softly. "I made you breakfast. I don't know what you like so I kept it simple."

You blink your eyes a few times, a look of disbelief shrouds your face. You sit up, your breasts are exposed, you pull the sheet up to cover yourself. You look over at the nightstand and see the tray of food waiting for you, then look at me.

A flood of emotions fills you, some still lingering from last night, still things feel new. Even the smell of the waiting food and coffee smells better than it has ever in the past. This kindness, the tender touches that this man has shown you in less than twenty-four hours is more than any man has done in the past. Small diamond-like tears start to form in your eyes. You cannot speak, or you may burst into tears.

I noticed the tears. I reach up and with my thumb I gently wipe them away. I could see the struggle that you were going through, my own heart melting.

"I should be going..." Is all that came out, but I wanted to somehow explain in words that do not exist that I understand and sorry for the turmoil that I placed you in. And that, if at all possible that I wanted, no needed to see you again.

Somehow you must have read my thoughts and said, "No! Don't go please stay." A small pause then you continued, "I'm sorry that I'm such a wreck right now."

I smiled at you and said, "That is good, I was thinking that you might hate eggs for breakfast."

You laugh at my attempt to lighten the mood. I smile at you.

"I like eggs." You say as you lean forward to kiss me. The sheet drops to your lap.

The kiss is long and passionate. We pull each other close and hold each other tight.

"You should eat before it gets too cold." I whisper in your ear. I struggle with letting you go, but I finally stand and hand you the tray.

I returned to the kitchen and started cleaning the mess that I made while preparing breakfast. A few minutes later I feel your arm wrap around me from behind. Your head resting on my shoulder.

"You don't have to do that, you cooked, I can clean." You tell me.

"I made this mess." A larger mess than should be for cooking eggs. I pick up your plate and start washing it.

I cannot see it, but I can feel that you are smiling again.

"I am going to take a shower. Would you like to join me?" You ask in a tempting tone.

I put the plate down to let it air dry and turn. You are wearing a sheer silk bathrobe; the tie strap is not tied. Your nipples are barely covered by the see-through material that drapes your lovely body.

Not even a gay man could resist this much temptation from such a beautiful lady. My mind lost, words were lost I could only utter, "Yes."

I follow you into the bathroom. You let the robe fall to the floor and you look back at me. I thought that the known limitations of what is beautiful and pleasing to the eye had just been shattered. A new standard of beauty stands before me, a new unattainable precedent for all things to fail at trying to achieve. All things once beautiful now dull in comparison to you.

You are facing the stream of water. I am behind you close, my hands washing your back.

Your skin so soft, that I am almost afraid to touch it with these old hands of mine as if my gentle touch would somehow scare this perfect canvas of art. But I cannot resist touching you.

You turn and tilt your head back to let the water flow through your hair, your fingers brushing the wet strands from your face and letting the stands fall behind you.

Your breasts are pushed closer due to you pushing your hair back. I lean down and take your nipple between my lips. You place one hand on the back of my head and pull me in closer. I take my other hand and start caressing your other breast.

The splash from the water raining down on you makes it almost impossible for me to look up at you. You notice this and move to the back of the tub. You lift one leg up and rest your weight of that leg on the edge of the tub.

Nothing in the history of mankind has anything ever been so inviting. A heroin addict would drop their syringe and never go back. You become my drug.

Instantly addicted from the first time I laid my eyes on you at the coffee shop.

I move in close looking up at you. You are licking your lips, then biting your lower lip when my hand touches your stomach. Deep breaths as I get closer and closer. You nod your head yes.

I bend down and I slowly lick your clit and apply slight pressure on your lower stomach with my raised hand. This makes you take quick inhales and fast exhales from my touch.

My tongue dances circles around your secret spot, not all was told last night, but no more secrets are to be had after this.

You can see the dancing figures again. They beckon you to dance with them. You remember the feeling last night, a once in a lifetime feeling. How could you ever experience that again?

My tongue dances to the sweet music of the water drops falling and the sighs of ecstasy that sing from your lovely lips.

You run to these figures of desire and again the embrace that consumes you. Warmth, a need fills you with what was had last night.

My tongue enters you; my hand rotates my thumb replaces where my tongue was, and it applies slight pressure with the same circling motion.

Your last secret from me is no longer. You taste like that of the finest white wine. The sweet hint of intoxicating grapes dance across my tongue. A blend of delicious flavors swirl around my kissing lips.

You can barely stand; you lower your body down into the tub. You kiss me you can taste yourself on my lips.

I stand and help you up. We finish our shower quickly because the water is starting to get colder by the second. I exit and start to dry off giving you some privacy to finish up.

You ask for a towel, I reach in and hand it to you. You step out drying your hair, only your face is covered by the towel. All the glorious beauty shimmering from your still wet skin shines for only I to see. I think to myself you have no idea what you are doing to me.

I had to leave the bathroom, or we would have to take a cold shower. You ask me on my way out, "Pick me out something to wear today."

I have never been asked that before, so I ask, "Anything in particular you like?"

Your answer, "Anything is fine."

I get dressed and walk to your closet. I am a jeans and t-shirt type of guy. I see that you have the same. I pick out a pair of jeans that I know will flatter your perfect ass, and long legs. Then a t-shirt with some print on it that of a child's cartoon movie; it had the words printed on it, 'To Infinity and Beyond.' I set the clothes on your bed and walk out.

I go back to the kitchen and finish cleaning and search again where to put away the clean dishes.

I head to the living room and notice an aquarium sitting on the table that I missed last night. A hand size tortoise was slowly crawling around.

"She is my best friend; I love her with all my heart." You say from behind me.

I turn around you are standing there naked, my eyes cannot move from your body, my mind is telling me to look away.

"Was there something wrong with what I picked out?" I asked looking down at my feet trying not to stare.

"Oh! No, just want to make sure that is what you wanted me to wear?" You ask.

I knew right then and there that I messed something up. No straight guy should ever be asked to pick out clothes for anyone. It is pure luck that some of us can even dress ourselves.

You smile and turn and walk back to your room. I headed back to the couch. 'Good job! Way to ruin a perfect start to a day. Why not the cute summer dress?' I think to myself.

You return and say, "Do you like?" As you spin all the way around.

'Should have picked the summer dress.' I thought again. I smile, "Of course, you could wear a paper sack and walk down the catwalk, and all fashion moguls would want to sell it in their stores."

You laugh, "You ready, more to see, and do, and culture to live." You say.

"May we stop at my hotel room first, so I can change into fresh clothes?" I ask, looking down at still clean clothes but with a disgusted face as if they were covered in mud.

"But of course." You answer. I could not place your tone in your voice. I was starting to worry.

49

At my hotel room I invite you in. You sit on the bed and do a little bounce like everyone else in the world does when they enter a hotel room, to check how soft it is. "I like this bed."

I smile and say, "It would be yours if mine to give."

I started to look for what I am going to wear. I pull out a shirt you shake your head no, a different shirt again a no, another a nod yes. I pull out a pair of pants a nod yes on the first try. I am smiling the entire time of this little game. I lay my cloths next to you, "I will be right back."

I go to the bathroom I brush my teeth, put on deodorant and freshen up as men do. I exit the bathroom taking off my shirt.

You are still sitting there, watching me, and removing your shirt. I could see what you were doing, mimicking what I was doing. I kick off my shoes, you do the same. I undo my pants, again you follow suit.

My pants are off and so are yours. I drop my underwear; you smile at me with a naughty smile. You are not wearing any panties; I could not believe that I did not notice earlier that you did not have a bra on either. I was so lost in how I ruined this day for picking out your clothes I did not notice.

"No panties?" I ask, knowing the answer.

"You did not pick a pair, so I thought you wanted me to go without." You say in a shy tone. You smile a devilish smile.

"I did not want you to think that I was some type of pervert going through your panties." I say in my defense.

You laugh, "I would have never thought that. Now come here." You tell me.

We are both naked. I walk towards you I lean in for a kiss, your arms wrap around my neck. I lean further slowly pushing you to the bed.

The graceful figure is there once again. You look around and you do not see the tiny flame, the campfire or the bonfire or the raging forest fire.

You hear a voice inside your mind, "Don't be afraid. You are confused, which is natural, and understandable." The voice is that of pure want and desire. "The spark which started the flame and grew larger, warmer is all still there. They are just beyond the raging fire of where you were reborn."

You say out loud, "I want it again."

I hear your words of desire as I am kissing your neck I whisper in your ear, "Soon."

Your world of fire and the world that you are lying in bed with a stranger are connected by a thin veil of reality.

The figure says. "Your mind has created this place, has created me; for reasons to help you understand."

You think, "Understand what?"

"You have had lovers in the past, and even cared for some of them deeply, but it was all for the pleasures of the flesh." The figure answers.

I am tracing your perfect curves with my soft kisses. Your hands are following, as if to push the after effects deep into your soft silky skin.

"Are you saying I am falling in..." The figure cuts your thoughts off with. "Everything starts at a single point then moves along a path of hundreds of possibilities, but only one point can be chosen. I do not know what point will be chosen next, any better than you do. What I can tell you is that you have a strong connection with this man, stronger than all that have come before, and possibly all that will come afterwards." The figure tells you.

I am at the edge of the bed I am kissing the inside of your thighs. Drawing closer to you. You reach down before my tongue can start dancing and pull me up to you and you say, "I want you inside of me."

"Tell me more, I need to know." You plead with the figure standing next to you.

You see the hints of a smile behind the flames of this figure; it is peaceful and calming. "All I can tell you is the next point lies ahead, and it is up to you to choose which way to move ahead." It tells you.

The figure reaches out its hand, you take its hand in yours; I enter you slowly, gently pushing in my full length. The warmth of the figure's hand warms your entire body. You cum on me while I am deep inside your tight pussy.

You lead the figure to this next point of this unknown line in this chain of events unfolding in front of you. Even in this world created by your mind you picture a row of doors that would represent all the possible choices, but there is nothing. "What choice do I have? What is the choice?" You ask your guide.

"It is simpler than you think. A step in any direction and the choice is made." The figure tells you.

"But I don't know the outcome." You demand an answer.

"No one ever does." The voice seemed to fade. You look at the figure as it fades to nothing. You are left alone with a choice to make. The thought of standing in front of the raging forest fire fills your mind and you remember the step away left you feeling cold and empty inside, and how the step forward brought you warmth, peace, and comfort.

You move up further on to the bed and roll to your side. I move to where my chest is facing your back. I enter you; you take a step forward.

A wall of flames appears, but not of that like the forest fire with the hues of yellows, reds, and oranges dancing. This wall of flames danced in colors of blues and whites. The heat is stronger than you have felt from any of the other fires. You know you can turn back, but this is new, this is exciting, you know what will happen if you walk into this beautiful fire at least you think you do.

You step closer and closer, again keeping in step with my thrust and the rocking of your hips. You reach into the wall, so close to burning heat, so close to pain, but something new a pressure, a building pressure on your hand.

You lean your upper body forward, staying in the same position and with one hand you lick three fingers. You reach back and start to massage your tight little ass. You touch my stomach with your fingertips; I slow to a stop.

You are taking deep breathes you reach down and remove my cock from you. You adjust your hips slightly downwards while raising your leg from the bed. I reach down and help support your lifted leg. You guide my cock to your forbidden place.

You feel the tip enter; you walk into the blue, white flames. Heat, pressure, and pleasure are all that you feel.

What escaped you was not a moan or a sigh of pleasure, I stopped. "No! Don't stop, just go slow." You say in quick gasps.

I push slowly. The flames have consumed you once again. Only your thoughts and pleasure remain. But this is somehow different, a more intense clarity of the mind. You can see the spark again that leads you to the forest fire, and all that lead you up to this point, but you can see past the spark and all the points of your life. All the single choices that lead to this moment. This unbelievable moment.

My thrusts are steady and slow. You remove your hand from my stomach and place it on your ass. You squeeze tightly and pull upwards and slowly start rocking your hips.

Even with your body gone the sense of heat, pressure and excitement keep building. It is unlike anything you have ever felt before. A tingle of fear creeps in that if it continues there will be nothing left of you, but you cannot bring yourself to stop.

My pace does not increase; not wanting to hurt you, but your rocking does.

There is nothing. No more heat, no more pressure building. Not even a thought. Silence surrounds you. There is no light, but wherever you are, it is not dark, nor is it white, it is clear. The silence is broken, after what seemed to be an eternity of peace. "You choose to move forward, remember all choices are yours to make." The figures voice said. You can see again it is standing next to you, different now, not the yellow, red, orange flames covering it, but now the blue, white flames danced it the other colors places. Your body returns.

I spill all my cum deep inside your tight ass. You lay there still, catching your breath. I slowly exit you. You turn over we kiss and lie there in each other's arms. We lay there for an hour or so, we do not talk, we just look in each other's eyes and that is all the talking we need at that time.

I move first you reach and take my arm and say, "A little longer."

I could not resist an angel making a request I obey or be damned to hell for all eternity.

"We should get something to eat." I say after a few minutes. You smile and nod your head yes. We both jump in the shower and only clean our bodies this time.

I put on my shoes then start picking up the room from my dirty clothes. You look at me and say, "Bring your stuff, you can stay with me, if you would like?"

I half expected to lift my head out of the books now. This cannot be happening especially to a guy like me. I ask, "What did you say?"

You repeat it more shyly this time thinking that I might not want to stay with you. You look down.

I walk up to you, reach up and lift your head up to look into your eyes. "I will, and thank you, this just seems too good to be true. I am waiting to wake up from a dream."

Your confidence is restored, and you kiss me then hug me.

I check out of the hotel. I place my bags in the boot of your car. You take us to a small restaurant. "This is my favorite Italian place to eat. You like Italian, don't you?" With worry in your voice.

"Love it." I smile to reassure you that anything you picked would have been my favorite.

We sit down order and start talking. Something was said that made us both start laughing at the end of the meal. We laughed and laughed we could not stop. We were laughing so hard we were about to start crying. The waiter even had to come over and ask us to keep it down as politely as he could. We could not stop. Our communication turned into pointing and hand gestures. We had to leave before we were asked to leave. I paid and tried to apologize for our behavior, but it all seemed that I was making a joke out of it.

Once outside and on the sidewalk, we let it all out. People walking by looked at us as if we were crazy, but we did not care. I try to catch my breath, heaving my words out, "We, better, go, before, some, one, calls, the, Bobbies, on, us!" This sends another wave of laughter through you.

You in the same heaving way say, "We, don't call, them, Bobbies," laughter "...we call, them, Police, like, you, Americans."

Our stomachs are sore from the laughter, our faces are hurting from smiling; but we continue to smile.

You drive us to a little spot by the beach. "I like coming here it helps me relax." You say in a calming voice.

Having lived by the ocean for nearly twenty years I know what you mean. "What is it that draws us to the Ocean?" Not asking but speaking a thought out loud.

"I think it is everything that it is. The calming, soothing sounds, the beautiful colors, the vastness, the depth, another whole world of life under the surface, and the raw power of it all." You answer my question.

I move closer to you I take one of your hands. You move it to your lap and hold it with both of your hands.

The blue, white figure is not there. You wanted to ask it so many questions, but only you stood there with the questions circling you. You try to think of one question and all the possible answers that could be given to that one question. The possible answers were as vast as the ocean that was in front of you. Shallow mixed with meaningful depth, elegant words of flattery, answers that could calm and relax your anxious mind and the destructive one that could break your very will.

You close your eyes and take a deep breath, clearing your mind of all the questions and answers.

Your mind is clear when the soft voice spoke, "You know that this will end; he will return home soon."

Your eyes pop open, you just realized that I would have to go home. You knew it, but now it struck you. A part of you already started missing me, even though we sat there shoulder to shoulder.

You turn slightly towards me, you look down searching for the right words, they are there you know what to ask, but afraid of the answer that you may hear. You slowly look up and say, "These past two days, from the coffee shop to sitting here with you right now, have been the best days I have had in my life. I don't want it to end; but I know that you must go back home. I'm not asking for anything, because I truly don't know what I want. If things were different, not so complicated then I may know what it is that I want." You stop.

I understood, I knew the meaning of every word and the words that were not spoken. The reason I knew was that I, myself, felt the same way, had the same thoughts.

I reach up with both hands and bring you in slowly and kiss you. A kiss of passion accompanied by the soft rolling waves landing on the beach. A cool summer breeze from the soothing ocean. The setting sun paints brilliant colors across the sky.

No movie, book, song or artist of any type could have captured a more perfect moment or dreamed of the place and time that you and I shared at that moment.

Time seemed to stand still. The outside world vanished. We were not just two people anymore, we were one and all.

The kiss ends slowly, eyes open just as slow, "I understand, and feel the same. I keep having this feeling that this is all a dream and any second I'm going to wake up and be forced to live in a nightmare." I tell you.

Tears start to form in your eyes an answer that you hoped for, wanted, needed; but the truth remains that I will have to leave.

I wipe the tears from your eyes and say, "Please don't cry, I am not pretty when I cry."

You start to laugh, your hand shots to hold your stomach still tender from our laughing fit from earlier.

"Stop that I'm still hurting." You say while pushing me playfully away.

We both smile and look back at the ocean; both seeking answers from its peaceful music and calming beauty.

You take my hand and lead us back to your car. We are back at your place you open the boot. I retrieve my bags and walk inside.

You take my things and place them in your room. Then come back to the living room where I am waiting for you. You turn on the television we sit and watch the show that you turned on. You lay your head in my lap. I do not understand what is going on in the program, so I watch you instead. I see your eyes get wide, the beautiful smile, even the shock of what is going on in this show all on your lovely face.

My hand is playing with your silky soft hair. I hear the music that ends the program. You look up at me and ask, "Did you like it; it is my favorite show to watch?"

"I did, and it is my favorite thing to watch as well." I answer truthfully.

You smile and say, "You were looking at me the entire time."

"I know and enjoyed every minute watching my favorite thing." I said.

The bashful giggle, "Stop." You again reach for your stomach. I reach down and place my hand on top of yours.

You roll to your back and look up at me. We are just looking at each other. Never has a creature of such beauty graced this earth before. You take my hand and place it on your stomach under your shirt.

My warm touch on your soft skin sends a slow exhale through our parted lips. My hand resting there on your flat stomach rises and falls with your slow rhythmic breathing. I smile.

"What?" You ask.

"I feel like I have won the lottery of life, of all the men in the world and I am here with you." I say to you.

You smile and lean up I bend down we kiss.

We get up and walk into your room. You slowly remove your clothing as I do the same. We crawl into your bed. Dare I say it? We made love.

The blue, white figure is there with you again. "Another path is open, find your way." It says, before it vanishes.

You take a step forward, you do not even think about it. A wall of flames of the perfect shade of purple. Never have you seen this hue. You want to run and throw yourself into it, and experience all the pleasures that it may have to offer; but you cannot run, the beauty of it, never have you seen such beauty in a single color. The humbling effects of the color brings tears to your eyes. You move closer to the wall. You cannot believe your own eyes; beauty becomes even more beautiful. You stop and stare, afraid to even blink for if you blink it may disappear and be gone forever. You push forward, you are arm's length from the wall of beauty, and what waits within.

The beauty of it is so strong you have to look away, no mortal eyes should ever see such perfection. You can feel a crushing force pushing you down. You are on your hands and knees. You look up at the wall, afraid that something else has taken it place, but the perfect beauty remains.

Tears are streaming down your lovely face. You crawl closer, you cannot look at the wall, your mind, no one's mind can fathom this type of beauty. It is not a piercing bright light that causes discomfort. It is a thing of such beauty that if all could see it would change the world forever. You steal a glance. Your eyes become wide, your pupils dilate, you are frozen. You will your body to move, but nothing happens.

The blue, white figure appears reaches down and picks you up. You feel the tender warmth of its touch as it cradles you in its arms. You feel helpless like a newborn baby dependent on others for all that you need.

"Do you want to move into the flames?" It asks.

With all your might you answer, "I need it."

The blue, white figure takes a step into the flames. Weightlessness, pleasure beyond belief courses through the very core of your being. Your body jumps and becomes ridged; you want to scream but nothing comes out. Your hands grasp for anything to hold you to this world the physical world, but nothing is found. You are gone.

Your head and shoulder, and the heels of your feet press hard against the bed. Your back arches upwards no longer touching anything but the air on your back. The sudden movement of your hips causes me to exit you and pushes me slightly back. Your arms are next to your side stiff, hands grasping at the sheets. Your head is tilted back, eyes roll, mouth open wide. You stay like this for no more than a few seconds, then fall hard back to bed.

I can hear your breathing choppy inhales, and quick short exhales. I see the tears streaking from the corners of your eyes. I move next to you, I touch your cheek to wipe away the tears.

"Don't!" You snap.

It was not that you did not want me to touch you. It was as if every nerve in your body was firing at the same time, hypersensitive to everything around you. The state that you were in you could swear you could feel every strand of hair growing. You start to shake the warmth fading from you and the air-conditioned air cooling your naked body. A shiver takes hold of you.

I pull the covers up over you. The touch and weight of the blanket is almost unbearable. I roll out of your bed, I look back, you swallow hard and say, "No. Please come back. I did not mean it that way. I just never..." You broke off the sentence before it was finished.

You reach out and take my arm you pull weakly, but it is all the strength that you have. I climb back into bed and move under the covers. I gently place a hand on your stomach. Your stomach jumps, you reach down to hold my hand in place before I can remove it. Your breathing starts to return to normal. A few shakes, and shivers still roll through your body while you are regaining control.

You take a deep breath and let it out slowly through your mouth. You turn to me and smile.

Each time I look at you I see an impossible thing, a beauty that keeps becoming more beautiful.

"I don't know what happened; I'm sorry." You say to me.

I raise my hand and put a finger over your lips. The touch makes you take a deep breath still, the feelings of hyper sensitivity lingers. You close your eyes. You still want me inside you. You reach down between your legs, your finger with the lightest possible touch to your clit; sends a lightning bolt streaking through your body. You let out a hushed whimper. You realize you are too sensitive to do anything else.

You embrace me holding me tightly. Tears start to form again. You think, 'What has this man done to me?'

Your eyes are getting heavy, the pleasure has drained you of all your energy, your mind is drained by all the emotions. You look at me with your amazing eyes, blinking slower and slower. I nod my head yes; you smile a tender smile back and nod your head. We close our eyes at the same time.

Chapter Three: Day Three Day Trip

I wake to the smell of coffee; my hand reaches out to find an empty bed. First thought, yes it was a dream too good to be true. I open my eyes; this is not my room. This is yours.

I see you walk in, you are dressed and holding a cup of coffee. You reach down and hand it to me. I thank you as I sit up. You smile. "I have something planned for us, if that is alright?"

I smile, "As long as I can spend time with your, then it will be perfect."

You lean in and kiss me on the cheek then said, "I laid you out some clothes." You smile a devilish grin.

I thought payback is fair play. I will be going commando all day. "May a take a shower, before the adventure begins?" I ask.

I get up out of bed, you are sitting there watching my naked body. I take a step towards the bathroom; I feel a slap on my ass. I turn with a jump from the unexpected touch not from the pain. I see you smiling and the giggle of perfect harmony. People image harps lightly being played in the halls of Heaven; after hearing your giggle I know this not to be true.

After my shower, I walk back into the bedroom. My clothes for the day are laid out on the bed. I see there is a pair of underwear. I laughed to myself.

I walk out of your room you are cutting up a cucumber and placing it in the aquarium for tortoise.

You look back and see me watching you. "Are you ready? I will be done here in a few seconds." You let me know.

I answer, "I will be ready." I turn and get the cup of coffee, drink it down, and take the cup to the kitchen. You were standing over the sink cleaning up.

I walk up behind you I reach around you with the cup in one hand to rinse it out. My other hand brushes your hair to the side to expose your neck. My lips kiss your neck softly. You tilt your head away allowing my kisses to explore more of your soft skin. You want the kisses to continue; you want pleasure. You think to yourself, Damn the plans.'

You turn around and say with wanting eyes, and desire in your voice, "We can stay here, order food in when we get hungry."

"That would be a dream come true, but you made plans for us. I would be one of those selfish 'blokes' if I agreed to that. So, my sweet angel let us be off and start this perfect day." I tell you.

I watched with my own eyes a pure sex goddess with an aura of desire, lust, craving, hunger and temptation melt away, with what I said. Left standing was an innocent young lady of love, caring, compassion, and tenderness. I could not say which was more beautiful.

The cup slips from my hand and hits the bottom of the sink. The sound is deafening in the silence. We both jump at the sound and start laughing. If the cup had not slipped from my hand, we would have never left. The universe works in mysterious ways.

England and America most of the spoken and written language is English. So, when we started driving, I was able to read the road signs and figured out where we were headed. The speed limit signs, and distances did throw me off a little bit.

You park in an all-day parking lot; you pay the attendant. We start walking down one of the hundreds of streets of London.

"Nowhere else will you find more culture than here while in England than London. It has everything to offer." You say to me as if you were a professional tour guide.

I smile at you and reach down to take your hand. You smile as you interlock your fingers with mine and we begin our adventure.

Old Ben, The Royal Palace, The Eye, London Bridge (which is not falling down), and landmark after landmark we walked. You would tell me what it was if I did not know and a little bit about it. In between landmarks we would talk about life, hopes, dreams, but we were careful with our words. A dread filled us both and it approached closer with each passing second.

We would jump into a few little bars to get a drink to cool ourselves down from the summer day, and the fast pace at which we were going.

In a single day I saw and experienced more of this beautiful culture than any other place that I have ever visited. You were no tour guide, but a true angel that blessed me with these gifts that I asked for not just two days ago. A lost soul if you will, now lead by the hand, out of the darkness and into the light by you an angel; dare I say my angel?

You break my thoughts with, "Are you O.K.?"

"Sorry I was lost again, and once again you save the day." I say with a smile.

You giggle, "What was that mind of yours thinking?"

"I was thinking that I would not have experienced a fraction of this in my five days here if it was not for you. The happiest days of my life before this trip are stale in comparison to this here and now." I tell you.

You start to blush and say, "How do you do it? Know all the right words and when to say them?" Wanting to know some secret or trick that only magicians know and keep hidden.

I look at you and say, "There is no trick; unless saying what, you believe to be true is some trick that I do not know about."

Your eyes go wide with shock and say in an excited voice, "Just like that!" You are pointing at me. "How did you know that I thought it was a trick?"

I start laughing and with a smile I say, "I promise you that there is no trick. Think about this, if something is too good to be true, then it must be. So, we try to find the trick behind it, but when something like this happens, the too good to be true moments in life, that we find ourselves in we can see that they are real, that they are true, and we want those moments no matter how small to last."

The shock fades from your beautiful face as a sign of understanding, and say, "You are right, I don't want this to end."

The voice, that sweet, kind, alluring voice, of the figure that picked you up and carried you into the beautiful flames softy whispers, "You are close to another choice." The voice was gone just as quick as it appeared, but it seemed that something was left unspoken.

You think, "What choice? What are you saying? Please tell me." You beg, but no answer is returned.

I answer you, "I don't want it to end either, but..."

"Let's not talk about that; there is still much to see and do." You say trying to block out that this is too good to be true, because it is going to end, but not by choice.

We continue until dusk and head back to your place.

"Let's stop and pick up some ice cream." I offer the suggestion.

You smile, "Ice cream?" You ask.

"Yes, everybody likes ice cream." I was about to do the little jingle, 'you scream, I scream, we all scream, for ice cream.' But stop myself with a little laugh.

We stop and I pick you up some dairy free ice cream. "I cannot remember the last time I had this." You say to me.

I smile and tell you, "I have it at least once a summer when I visit my sister and niece. We have a movie night and only snack foods."

You smile, "That sounds amazing."

"It really is, my sister even though she is younger than me is my rock, she keeps me grounded. I would not know where I would be without her, and I would never let her know what I just said either. I tell you a family secret.

You imagine in your mind what it would feel like, a family sitting, laughing, enjoying the time that they have with each other. You can see the entire room from where you are sitting. You see a lady and a young lady sitting on a couch. You see me sitting on a love seat, and you are sitting next to me holding my arm, head resting on my shoulder, you can smell the room, taste the snacks, and hear my heart beating. You felt welcomed and happy.

The voice returns, "The choice is now." Quiet again. You are alone, no doors of infinite possibilities, just a step in any direction to choose your fate. You quickly think back, step back the cool chill, step forward beauty and pleasure, and each step forward has always proved to be greater than the last. You cannot image anything more powerful than the purple flames that you had to be carried into, by sheer will, the blue, white figure of your mind. You want to step forward and face the fear of the unknown. You raise one leg slowly in front of you. Your heart starts pounding in your chest, your breathing becomes faster and faster. Your leg continues to rise, you begin to lean forward. You let gravity make your choice for you. You are at the tipping point of falling forward.

Half expecting not to be able to even look at what lies ahead of you when your foot touches down. You feel the point that your balance and gravity are fighting for control, small sways back then forward, again, and again. You let gravity win.

You walked inside and brought out two spoons. We are sitting outside enjoying the clear night looking up at the stars and the half-moon. You take tiny spoon full, and let it melt in your mouth. You smile at the sweetness. I reach up to kiss you. The flavors mix as we kiss, with the sweeter taste of your lips. Pure umami, the Japanese word for perfect taste.

Your raised foot falls in front of you. You wait the spilt second for it to find solid ground, even though your heel of your other foot is off the ground, and your other leg is pushing you forward. The ground is not there. Gravity, has it held, the choice was made, and there is no way of stopping it now. You inhale deeply as you start to fall.

The kiss ends slowly; you take a deep breath. You feel yourself falling, you try to think what did this to you, 'The ice cream, the kiss, the sex, the kind words, this American, or was it everything?' Your rational mind tries to stop the descent, but even the power of the rational mind can never overpower the feelings of the heart.

I can see a subtle change in your eyes, a new softness, a new tenderness sparkles there. A picture of paradise flashes in my mind. Lush vibrant colors, cool breeze, a warm sun, a day bed on a beach, pure white bedding and you there laying on top beckoning me to join you.

I stand up and hold out my hand, you take it we walk inside.

You walk into the living room, and you turn on some music. The song is slow, I place one hand around your waist, the other takes your hand. I step close. You rest your head on my shoulder, as we shuffle our feet slowly to the music.

"Is there nothing that you cannot do?" You asked me.

"I feel like I can do anything and everything when I am with you." I whisper back.

Another slow song we continue to slowly move with the beat. Notes filling the air we could have danced this dance the rest of the night, but all songs come to an end.

The next song one from the eighties' an up-beat tone. We both smile because we know it and start jumping to the beat waving our arms around throwing our heads this way and that way. The pure enjoyment that you are having shows through your smile and your eyes. The song ends, we are both out of breath, but we keep going. Our moves do not match you go up; I go down. You move left at the same time as I move towards my left. Any person that could see us would know that we were fools, but we would not care let them think what the will.

The song ends we cannot do another we sit and laugh at each other and with each other.

You get up and shortly return with two glasses of wine. We are sitting there just smiling. It is like our own bodies forgot how to do any other expression but that of a smile.

A seductive song starts to play, I start to stand about to ask for another dance, when you stand, and push me back down to sit. You start with your back to me moving your hips to the beat back and forth. You arch your back then roll into a standing position all while looking back at me, licking your lips, and slowly blinking your eyes. Your hands brush your hair upwards and let it fall where it may, your hands start caressing every inch of your body while they make their way down your tempting body.

You bend at the waist keeping your legs straight and slightly apart, again you arch your back, hands are on your ankles and your hands move up as your roll to the standing pose again, this time your hands take hold of the sun dress you are wearing and lift, until it is up and over your head. You are still moving to the music I lean forward you raise a hand and with one finger you shake it side to side. I stop, not even the strongest man alive could resist or disobey a command from a goddess. I fell back in place.

You reach up with both hands and unclasp your bra, you drop your shoulders, and the straps slide off your silky skin. With one hand and forearm your cover your nipples as you turn to face me.

You take a step forward, nudge my leg with your knee, you open a pathway to move in closer. You lean down, you remove your arm from covering your perfect breasts, your hands are on my shoulders pinning me to the back of the couch. You lean in and place your breasts in my face, I kiss as they slide up and down, left and right. My hands start at your wrists and slowly slide upwards to your shoulders; I was about to pull you on top of me when you pull away and slowly turn and take a step away from me.

The sense of falling has been there this entire time, but now there is something next to you. You look, and you want to know how it is possible that you are looking at yourself. "You always knew. The desire, excitement and passion all burn inside you. If you were able to see yourself dancing in these flames before going in on your own free will, you may have never made the choice to continue down the path that you are on." You answer your falling self.

Your falling self says, "I can see that you are me, but you are so much more beautiful than I am."

You giggle at the falling you, you hear the true music of the sound. "You are not just seeing what you see with your own eyes. You are seeing what he sees in you as well, not just the pleasing frame, surrounded by soft silky flesh; but he sees the kindness, tenderness, your intelligent mind, your drive, wants, dreams, hopes, fears, love and everything else; he sees the beauty within, even if you cannot."

You lean down and sit on my lap, you look back, you are watching me enjoy the show. You gyrate your hips, you smile, you can feel me becoming hard.

You stand back up and slowly push your panties to the floor, you take a step and kick your panties to the side. You slowly turn as your hands move again one to cover your wanting pussy, the other in the same hand bra as before. Your hips have not stopped the seductive movements the entire song.

The song is on its last few beats. You move in close to me, no two people on Earth could be this close without touching.

You ask, "But, why him? He has to leave."

"We do not pick and choose who we fall for, or when, or place, it just happens. The choice you made is allowing yourself to fall. I am sorry, all things must come to an end, enjoy every single moment of time that you do have." You say to the falling you.

With the end of the song, you let your body fall the millimeter that separated us from touching, you kiss me, I kiss you back. We are like hungry animals, tearing at my clothes to get them off.

You see a tiny speck of light below you, a quick thought enters your mind; HELL! A hell without me, but as quickly as the thought entered it is erased by the familiar warmth of the raging forest fire.

My clothes are scattered throughout the room; you are sitting on my lap you can feel my hard cock pressing against your clit. You reach down, lift your hips, and slide me inside you.

The fire raging in yellows, reds and oranges has filled your entire sight as you fall closer and closer to it. You outstretch your arms tilt your head back as you fall into the flames of desire.

You raise and lower your hips faster and faster until you rest with the full length of my cock inside you. Your breathing is fast, you smile and start again, a little faster this time.

Through the flames of desire, you fall, and as fast as you ride my cock the faster you fall. You see another speck of light shines below you. You know what this is and want it, the flames of excitement.

Even though falling through the flames of desire seemed like a moment, in comparison to the first experience the effects were just intense, more so if that is even possible.

I push you to the side and roll you to your back. Your head is resting on the lower back support part of the couch, your chin almost touching your chest. Your back on the seat of the couch, and your hips and legs are totally off the seat.

I stand, step in between your legs. I reach down with each arm and pick up your long legs, lifting them higher than your back resting on the seat of the couch. You wrap your legs around me; I thrust inside of you.

From this position my cock finds new hidden pleasure spots that only you knew about; you fall faster.

You start massaging your breasts, you slowly start tightening your grip around my waist the closer you get to the blue, white flames.

You do not know how you are able to continue. The first time the flames of desire had you spent. The first time in the flames of excitement the same. What is driving you? The fall through the flames of desire should have ended the session, the same pleasure, same warmth was there. Is it the falling that is letting yourself go beyond or is it your will power to see the beautiful flames of passion again? You do not know the answer, but whatever it maybe you do not want it to stop.

The closer that you get to the blue, white flames of excitement you can feel the pleasure pushing around you, the pressure squeezing you lightly.

You look up at me, you are panting through parted lips. You squeeze your own breast; you pull one close to your mouth. You kiss your own breast. You squeeze harder.

The blue, white flames are all that you can see. The pressure is building. You picture how a diamond is formed. Pressure, heat and time that turns coal into a valuable stone, that represent love and forever. You feel your core turn into that diamond.

The moment that you enter the flames the pressure shifts, not pressing from the outside anymore. A pressure from within. The diamond is expanding, sending out rays of warm light through your body. The pleasure of me inside of you continues to grow. You feel that you will explode. You take a deep breath; you let your body relax for the briefest of moments. You feel me find that hidden spot.

Your hips buck and rock hard against me, no moan or sigh but a tiny scream of pleasure. Your teeth are clinched, breathing heavy, whipping your head side to side. I stop in fear of hurting you.

"Don't stop! Keep going!" You demand.

I obey and push hard and fast inside of you. I try to keep up with your rocking hips. One of your legs slips from my grip, it falls to the floor tilting your hips slightly, as we both thrust our bodies together. An audible slapping sound from flesh hitting flesh can be heard.

You squeeze your breasts hard, the one leg that I am still holding squeezes and pulls me deeper inside of you. The diamond shatters and flies throughout your body. Not even the strongest stone could contain this pleasure. Pleasure spills out as burning blue, white flames. Your body consumed by it only your thoughts are falling now.

You relax; I slow my pace. You take one of your hands and slowly rub your clit while I am still preforming. You reach up with your other hand and touch my stomach with your fingertips.

I feel your gentle touch I know you want or need me to stop. It takes all my power to do just that.

I slowly lower your leg; you sit up and pull me by my hips. My cock still wet from being inside you, and you take it in your mouth. My head tilts back my hands find hold of the side of your bobbing head.

I look down at you, you look up at me. I can see it in your eyes you want my cum in your mouth. I shake my head no. A flash of hell for all eternity enters my mind for not granting this beautiful angel's wish. I reach down and take you by the arms and lift. You stand; I lead us to the bedroom.

Your thoughts are still falling, but you still have all your senses. You could taste yourself on my cock, you felt my touch when lifting you up, you could hear my heart pounding, you could even smell the sweet scent of sex in the air, and now you could see the beautiful purple flames of passion.

We are standing in front of the bed. I turn to you, I see perfection. I step closer to you and kiss you tenderly. I pour every emotion that I have into this kiss, hoping somehow, some way you will be able to understand how I feel for you.

Not knowing if the message sealed in a kiss was received but it seemed that you did the same. The kiss ends, both drunk from the intoxicating kiss, eyes open slowly. You climb into bed, I follow.

The beauty of the purple flames is so intense you wish that you could look away but cannot. I enter you slowly, tenderly, you fall into the purple flames.

Tranquility.

Your eyes open, your body has returned and still falling. Passing through the flames of passion just as intense as the first time when you were carried by the blue, white figure. You half expect yourself to offer some cryptic advice on choices but instead you feel a touch on your hand, you turn and look.

Your beautiful eyes widen, a smile that ends all hate fills your lovely face. You see me falling with you.

We make love for the rest of the night, until we pass out in each other's arms.

Chapter Four: Days Four and Five

I wake you are still sleeping, peacefully, a dream come true. There is something that I must do, something in the back of my mind. How I wanted to just lay here watching you sleep.

I slowly get out of bed trying not to wake you. I found a few sheets of paper and a pen. I sat down and started writing. On the first sheet I wrote down all the possible ways that you will be able to contact me. The other two just words.

I leave my contact information on the little table in the kitchen, potted plants at the edge near the window. I fold the other two sheets of paper neatly and place them in a side pocket of my bag. I crawl back into bed.

"Everything alright?" You ask, in a sleepy voice. Your back is to me, which I was thankful for.

I leaned in and kissed your shoulder, and with tears forming in my eyes I say, "Everything is fine my angel."

Your hand reaches back and gently touches my check. I blink away my tears as you roll over to face me.

My last full day; four days of a living soul walking the halls of heaven, basking in the glorious light, and warmth. I now know what true peace, comfort, and serenity is. A place that is safe, kind, and tender what one should feel like, as they enter, home.

You say, "For a man that has traveled the seven seas, and circled the globe, you get lost a lot." You smile.

"I can stay lost in your eyes, knowing that you will find me and lead me back to you." I say.

You crawl on top of me. Eyes lock. You can feel me getting hard. You slowly move your hips back and forth. Your clit is being rubbed against my shaft. Your hands are on my chest you begin to squeeze.

You think to the point of passing through the purple flames it must have been a dream that you thought you saw me falling with you.

Your mind jumps from that thought to one of searching. Trying to remember the last time this falling took hold of you.

There you see all the points of your life, you find one, a memory, a fond one, it is like watching a movie the entire experience watched in a blink of an eye, but no falling like this. Another point and the same, and both seemed to be growing out of focus.

Then you see the point sitting there with me eating ice cream. You can see the moment that you take the step and will fall. You tell yourself, "Yes, take the step."

The past experiences were real, deep caring emotions. You had the butterflies in your stomach fluttering around, and they gave you flight to walk amongst the clouds, but they were not strong enough to keep you there and while you watched them these memories seemed too dull.

Yes, the butterflies are in you now, they are in a frantic fight against the force that is pulling you. You can see their beautiful wings flapping, some are trying to glide, anything to slow your fall. Your heart goes out to them knowing nothing can stop this force, after you took that step. You open yourself up and let the butterflies fly free. They circle around your falling body. Such peaceful beauty. Some land on your hands, arms, and legs, they try again to slow your fall. You smile at these kind, loving creatures and tell them, "Be free, I will be alright." They listen to your command, and you fall away from them.

Your mind goes back to the moment of the fall, you relive that last second before it all starts. In slow motion you feel yourself fall; your mind's eye is trapped inside of your falling body.

You slide your hips further up; you reach down and guide my cock inside you while you slide your hips down.

You are falling. Your mind's eye is reliving the start of the fall the feelings are too intense your mind is becoming dizzy from two instances of falling and the pleasure of me being inside you.

A gentle pull brings your mind back to your falling body. You look in the direction of where the tug came from. I am there. You think 'it was not a dream.' You pull me close we embrace; we kiss as we continue to fall.

Our falling bodies tangle together, just as our bodies tangle in the physical world.

You look down and you see the raging fire below, you wonder if I had the same sensations, feelings, or is this new for me. My voice whispers in your mind, "New, yes, first time feeling the flames no."

You ask, "New? Not first time, what do you mean?"

"The flames, started with a spark, and continued to grow to a raging fire, pushing further pass to more raging fires, until I started to fall. But, now falling with you this is new; these fires only started when I met you, saw you sitting there at the coffee shop." I explain.

We fall through the flames of yellows, reds, and oranges. Holding each other tight, our bodies melt away, our minds become one. My thoughts become yours, yours become mine. We think at the same time how the world could be, should be if they could feel what we are feeling now. Not the pleasures of the flesh, but the emotions of this bond. The world would stop fighting, stop judging, work together, no more separation due to race, religion or country of origin, we would become just one race: Humans.

Our physical bodies working on pure instinct while our minds, our souls if you will, become one falling together, the pleasure of the flesh so intense, nothing is hidden, dreams, wants, and hopes all shared as we enter the blue, white flames.

Four days and we have become closer than that of an elderly couple that has been together for fifty years. We have no secrets, and even the deep hidden secrets we want to keep even from ourselves are revealed. No shame, no judgement, only understanding and compassion.

Neither of us remember moving but we are in the kitchen. You are leaning over the sink and the water is running. I am behind you with my hands on your shoulders both of us thrusting our bodies towards each other.

We are only thoughts now falling. We picture a perfect world like the Garden of Eden where all live-in peace. Where something as beautiful as making love is not looked down upon, but celebrated, and not like that of a Roman orgy. Freely expressed, the beauty of the body worshipped as it should be a blessing from God.

I could only assume that we moved from the bedroom to the kitchen for water, to quench our thirst and or to cool our bodies. Since two glasses of water are half full on the floor next to us in the living room.

I am sitting up right; you are sitting on my lap. Your breasts pressed hard against my chest. Your arms around me pulling me closer to you as my arms are doing the same. Your head tilted up, I am kissing your neck. Your hips slowly and ever so slightly move up and down.

The flames of passion raise up to meet our one mind. An explosion. We both can see how everything from the star millions of light years away is connected to a single dust particle from a moth's wing. The complexities of it all, and how simple it all was at the same time. We were everywhere and nowhere, we were everything and nothing all at the same time, an eternity in the smallest measurement of time.

You feel the first shot of cum inside you; you lower your hips and rest with my cock deep inside you as I fill you with the rest of my cum.

Neither of us can move. After a few minutes I lean back, I am still inside of you; you lean with me. I move to exit you.

"No stay inside me as long as you can." You ask me.

You can feel my once hard cock becoming soft, and retracting. When by nature and not by choice I exit you, we lay there kissing, holding each other for a least an hour.

We move to the shower we wash each other. Once finished we dry off but do not get dressed. You order food to be delivered.

A knock on the door, you in a cotton bathrobe answer. The young boy sees you he looks at you from head to toe, undressing you with his eyes. You roll your eyes and let out a huff as you pay, then close the door.

You come back to the living room, set down the food undo your robe and let it fall to the floor. Your naked body a glorious sight to see. You say, "The nerve of that boy, to look at me like that trying to undress me with his beady little eyes. What is wrong with men?"

As I, myself look at you from head to toe. You look down and see that I was doing the same thing the delivery boy did to offend you. You smile and sit.

"I know men are such pigs." I say, including myself in the grouping.

You lean in close and say, "I do not mind when you do it." You kiss me.

Our food was gone in minutes we did not realize how hungry we were. We sit on the couch talking and holding each other.

I get up and pick up the containers and throw them away. I pour two glasses of wine and return. You turned on some music. We sat there talking sipping the wine.

You lean your head on my chest listening to my heart. You place a hand on yours they are beating in rhythm. You think, 'True intimacy is not when we were making love, it is this moment, this calm, this peaceful moment. Where we hold each other in silence and smile at the memories.'

I look down and see your hand over your heart, I place mine on top of yours. "Connected somehow?" I say with a smile.

"You feel it too?" You ask.

"Yes." I lean down to kiss you.

I ask, "Is there anything that you want to do today?" The entire morning is gone, and half of the afternoon has already passed.

You look up at me with a smile and say, "Yes." You sit up and crawl on my lap and say, "Be with you." We kiss.

Time is funny, it seems to slow or speed up during certain events but always stays constant. When you want a moment to last and it is over way to fast, and when you want to be out of a situation time seems to stand still. Well, this is my experience at least, but now that I do not want this to end, and neither do you time seemed to speed up even faster.

Before we even realized it, it was two in the morning. We were not tired we were living or striving off of the pleasure each was giving. It was a give and take, but more intimate an offering and receiving of the body to the other.

We did fall asleep, but we did not know what time that might have been, but we slept holding each other on the couch.

My cell phone alarm goes off, I look at it, six hours before I need to be at the airport. I move gently not to wake you. I start a pot of coffee and go to my bag. I pull out the folded sheets of paper, I find an envelope and place them inside. I write your name on the outside. I place the letter to you under your pillow on the side of the bed where you normally sleep. I pull out my clothes and jump into the shower.

I make two cups and bring them to the living room where you are still sleeping. I sit on the floor. I watch you for a few seconds. Such peace, such beauty, wishing that I could see what beautiful dream you are dreaming. I gently place my hand on your cheek; you smile while still sleeping. My heart melts. Your hand reaches up and takes mine. You roll it over and kiss the back of my hand. Your eyes, your beautiful, thoughtful, caring eyes open slowly. A bashful smile appears on your lovely face.

"Coffee?" I ask already, ready for you.

"You are a God Send." You say, in a sleepy voice.

"No. Only a humble servant to you, my Goddess." I tell you.

Another bashful smile as you take the cup from my hand. A small sip, you smell the aroma, you feel yourself ready for the day. Then it hit you, I am leaving today. A weight drops upon you, that you cannot get out from under.

Your eyes get wide, "What time is it?" Worry in the lovely voice of yours.

I try my best to calm you only God knew that I was going through the same thing as you. I say, "We have plenty of time."

You jump up almost spilling the coffee, you rush into the bathroom. I hear the shower start as I walk in. You pick out your clothes and run back into the bathroom.

I sit on your bed next to the hidden letter. Wanting to give it to you now, it would explain everything, but I left it there.

You come back into the room, your hair is still wet, beads of water still tracing your curves. I stand and embrace you. I can feel some of the weight lift from you. "Please calm down, we still have some time." I say trying my best to ease your worried mind.

I take the towel and start drying you off, patting you, long gentle swipes of the soft towel down your arms, down your back, and down your long legs.

You stand there feeling helpless as I dry your lovely body. You want to say something, anything, everything but all words seem to be foreign to you. You take a deep breath and let it out slowly, calming yourself a little.

You get dressed as I pack my things.

"There is one place that I would like to go before I head to the airport, would you join me?" I ask.

"Anywhere you want..." You say, and you wanted to continue but the words would not come out.

With my bags over my shoulder, my hand in yours, we walk down this street and that street. I see in your face that you know where we are going, you wipe away small tears from your eyes.

I set my bag down at a small round table, I pull the chair out for you. You sit; your eyes are filling up with tears. I bend down and kiss the top of your head. I could not say anything. I walk inside, wiping tears of my own.

"American, you are back. What can I do you for today?" The lady said, remembering me.

I looked from the window to the lady. She must have seen the redness in my eyes. "Two coffees please." I say while clearing my throat.

"I see that you found what you were looking for." She says looking out the window at you.

"Yes, and so much more, but I have to return home." I say trying with all my might to fight the tears.

She nods and can see my personal struggle. She places the cups on the counter; I try to hand her the money. She waves it off. "On the house." I could not even say thank you to this kind lady, all I could do is nod a slight bow of my head.

I walk up behind you, I lightly tap your shoulder and say, "Excuse me Miss."

A jump, lost in your thoughts, you quickly remember the same exchange, you smile, and giggle, but with tears in your eyes. I set your coffee in front of you.

You think, 'How can this stupid little coffee shop be so romantic at a time like this.'

Tears again, "I'm sorry, it is I do not want you to leave." You said it, but the weight was still there.

I reach to take your hand. "I don't want to go."

We sit and try our best to talk, but something holds back what we really want to say to each other.

We walked to the train station, I turn to you about to say my good byes. You say, "I am going to the airport with you."

I smile and say, "Thank you."

I bought a round trip pass for you and a one way for me. It struck me hard. I will not be coming back with you. My heart fell into my stomach.

I hand you your pass. We board the train. You rest your head on my shoulder we do not say much, both lost, we both need each other to find our way now.

We arrived at the airport. You walk with me as far as you can. We hug each other tight. We kiss. We both dry each other's eyes. We want to say it, we want it to be real, if we say it aloud then it will be real, but neither of us speak the words. We know it in our hearts, minds, bodies, and souls that we do.

I searched for words that would convey what you mean to me and not sound inattentive to your feelings, but only 'thank you, I enjoyed my time...' entered my brain. What a guy thing to say, to a beautiful lady that showed me a world of beauty. I start to speak. You place a finger over my lips. You could sense that I was lost again, and once again saved me from my own self.

I reach in to kiss you. We could not hold it in we spoke at the same time, "I..." The loudspeaker broke our sentence off, "Thirty-minute warning for boarding passengers for flight..." It was my flight.

I kiss you again, you see the tears in my eyes, "I have to go." I turn, it takes all my might to turn away from you, as I step up to the customs booth.

"Do you have anything to declare?" The man asked.

'I do, that I am leaving the woman that I love standing alone.' I thought but said, "No."

You are much stronger than I, you return to your home with only a single tear falling along the way. Was it the shock that I was gone, was it the memories that helped you get home?

You stood there and look around your flat, it seemed smaller. You see something on the floor; you pick it up it is a shirt of mine that was missed when I was packing. You raise it to your face; you can smell me on it. You fall to the floor; tears, sobbing, you feel that part of you is missing.

You pull yourself together, and you just want to go to sleep. Sleep the rest of the day away. You lie down on your bed. You reach under your pillow to pull it close to you to hold, but your hand touches the letter I left for you. You pull it out from under your pillow.

You sit up. You look at it, you see your name written on it. You try to think when I could have done this, we were together the entire time.

You look down at my shirt and back at the letter. You carefully open it. You look over it quickly. You smile and think, 'There is nothing that I could not do.' You see a beautiful penmanship of cursive writing. You start to read.

To My Angel of England,

I do not know what state you will find this letter in, but I do have some idea. Please dry your crying eyes, you know that I am not pretty when I cry.

I want you, no; need you to think of the Italian restaurant, when you think of me. Let that time bring a smile to your lovely face for the whole world to see, for I will be doing the same. If that is not enough to ease your mind, picture us together at the beach. Remember the music of the waves, the vastness of it all, and the beauty of that moment.

How I prayed and searched for anything that could have changed this outcome, so I would not have to write this letter to you; to be there with you, to hold you, to kiss you one last time.

I cannot speak for you, I know only what my heart is telling me to be true. If you had said those three little words, I would not have left, and if I had spoken them you would not have let me leave.

My time with you, a treasured gem of perfection, a place in time to relive when I feel lost, and know that you, an Angel, will always lead me back.

My heart feels empty while writing this, even though you lie sleeping in the next room, because of the nature of this letter. But when you wake my heart will be filled and over flowing with joy and love.

I do not know how to describe the way I am going to miss you. The emptiness, sadness, being alone walking in a world of shadows, still does not tell you the way I will feel when I step on that damned plane to take me home.

My trip here was to live in the culture and embrace it. You gave that to me and so much more. You opened your home, showed me places that are not on any map; your kindness, tenderness, your gentle touch, your sweet kisses, your mind, the true you. For that I am forever in your debt.

I could write a novel just on what we shared while I was here with you, to describe every detail, every emotion, and every touch, but that is between you and me. But I feel that I am leaving something out of this letter, a magical phrase that will make these feelings easier to bare. There is no trick, only speaking the truth.

I have never been so happy in my life to be lost, for it led me to you. A beautiful young lady drinking a cup of coffee that I fell in love with the moment I saw you.

With Love always and forever; To Infinity and Beyond,

Your American.

You are filled with so many emotions, you press the letter against your chest and fall back into bed. You reach down and pull my shirt on top of you. You smile, you think of the restaurant, the beach, and all the other moments we shared, you close your eyes and fall asleep.

Chapter five: Returning Home

My gate is close I have plenty of time to board the plane. My mind was absent, my soul adrift in the massive empty universe, and my body felt invisible hidden from the world, as I walked towards the gate.

I did not even see the elderly man when I walked straight into him. I knocked his walking cane out of his hand with the impact.

I looked up in horror of what I just did, I reached down and picked up his cane, "I'm so sorry, are you alright?" I asked.

He looks up at me. I see his soft blue eyes, still filled with life and wisdom. "It is good to run into a fellow American, well not as hard as that." He said with a little chuckle. He looked up at me and his brow dropped slightly. He turns to his wife and without saying a word she smiles and walks over to the row of chairs that lines the walkways. She sits and then pats the chair next to her, inviting us to sit with her.

I help him to the seat, and he sits next to his wife. He tells me that they have been married for fifty-three years and never have been happier.

I could see that they still looked at each other like it was the first time. I could see the love that they had for each other. I could not help but smile, and tears fell from my eyes.

The lady placed a hand on her husband's shoulder and patted it with her fingers. He looked at her, then at me and saw my tears, he spoke, "Ahh! You are leaving but found something so powerful that where you call home, it would feel more like a prison. That is why you are lost to the world."

I nodded my head yes, unable to speak.

He looked at me with those knowing blue eyes and asked, "What is back there that you call home?"

"My elderly father, family, friends, school." I was able to choke out without balling my eyes out.

He turns to his wife, and asks, "They have schools here in England, don't they?" He asked as if he did not know. She smiled at him and nodded her head yes. He turns back to me and asks me a question, "Does your family and friends love you?"

A simple reply is what I gave him, "Yes."

He tells me that he met his wife in 1960, he was in the Army stationed here in England. One day after some of his friends and he was off duty they went out into town all dressed in crisp uniforms to impress the local towns people. He was describing every detail like it was yesterday. He said with a smile, "I saw an Angel sitting with a group of friends at a soda fountain café. I had to meet her, so I mustarded all the courage and confidence that I could and made my way towards her. The thing was I was so caught up in her beauty that I did not notice the tiny step. I tripped right in front of her, not a stumble and regaining my balance, but a fall straight to the ground. I wanted to run and never show my face again in this town. She, this beautiful angel, looked down, wide eyed, and started to giggle as she asked if I was alright. I looked up and started laughing. Ever since that day I have been falling for her every day."

He told me that they married two months later. They have two children, five grandchildren, and one great grandchild. He left the Army and stayed here in England, he left his family, friends, had no job, but he knew that he could not leave his one true love.

I understood what he was trying to tell me. I said, "But my father..."

He stops me with saying, "He is well enough for you to be here now. I am sure that he wants his son to be happy, don't you?"

I say, "True."

He changed his approach by asking, "What made you go back to school?"

It made my mind shift gears and think of something different. I answered, "I retired from the Navy, and it is time for something new."

He laughed and said, "I figured a sailor. Sailor of old sailed the oceans just using the stars. An amazing feat they always seemed to find their way home. Now my question to you is: which way are your stars telling you where home is?"

I looked towards his wife, she was smiling at me, the kindness in her eyes lifted the fog that was surrounding me.

The old man continued, "When you get to her, hug her, kiss her, then call your family and let them know."

I looked up and I could see the plane backing out of the gate. I felt a huge weight lifted. I said, "I missed my flight. I missed my flight!" Not with the upset dread, but with relief and thanking God excitement.

I stood up and kissed his wife on the cheek and took the old man's hand in mine and shook it saying, "Thank you, thank you so much." Tears of joy in my eyes as I started to leave the elderly couple.

"One more question, it was the giggle, wasn't it?" He asked smiling, most likely remembering his wife giggling at his tumble the first time they met.

"It was." I told him.

"It will get you very time." He told me. He raised his hand and waved it to shoe me off to go to my true love.

I started running. I ran out of the airport to the train station. While on the train I thought to myself that I could have run faster than the train was going. My heart was pounding. I have never done anything like this in my life. 'What are you going to think?' I asked myself. It was too late now.

The second the train stopped I was at a full sprint. I ran past the coffee shop, which brought a smile to my face even though I could barely catch my breath. I ran down this street dodging people, I ran down that street jumping out of the way of people walking their dogs.

I stopped in front of your flat. I must rest to slow my heart before it explodes and catch my breath. I lean down with my hands on my knees taking deep breaths.

You have moved to the right position on your bed your head is on the pillow. The letter still held close, your other arm holding another pillow. You are covered with my shirt.

You are dreaming that we are sitting on the couch watching a film and hear a knock on the door. You look at me, you were not excepting anyone. I shrug my shoulders, I do not know who it could be.

We let it be and continue to watch the film. Another knock, louder this time. You stand frustrated at the intrusion, you answer the door and I am standing there. You look back and I am sitting there waiting for you to come back. You look back at the door. Another knock even louder.

You open your eyes, the dream haunting you with knowing that I am in the air flying home. You try to think of the restaurant, the beach, but the tears are blurring even your thoughts.

You hear the knock. You want to crawl under the covers and hide, but the frantic way the knocking was it must be important.

You walk to the door, the letter still held close to your chest, and the other hand holding my shirt. You unlock the door and open it slowly. You look through the cracked door to see who could be banging on your door.

You see me standing there. Sweat running down my face. "No! Another Dream!" You shout.

I reach in and take hold of you in a loving embrace, and say, "Yes, a dream come true."

"But your flight, your family?" You ask.

"If I need to, I can get another flight, my family is still my family." I reached in and kiss you. You stand there in shock. You think, 'That I am giving up everything to be with you.' The shirt you were holding drops to the floor; tears form in your eyes you kiss me back.

"I know that there is so much that we need to talk about, but I have to make a phone call first." I tell you. You nod your head yes.

"Hello! Dad, it's me. This has to be quick, and I will explain later, but I am staying in England." I say when he answered.

"Everything alright?" He asked.

I look at you and say to my Dad, "Better than alright. I have to go."

"Alright then, be safe and have fun. I love you." He said with his regular closing.

"Love you too, Dad." I tell him as I hang up the phone.

I take your hand and lead you to the couch. You sit, you still cannot believe that I am here and then telling my Dad I was staying here. I sit and face you. I tell you everything from the point of the custom's booth, the old man's story, watching the plane pull away and how it made all sense, and how I ran here.

"I ran towards my star; my star that led me home; my home is any place where you are. I feel safe, at peace when I am with you. I love you." I say. These words did not even come close to describing how I feel for you, but I said it, said it out loud. I made this thing, this thought, this feeling, I made it real and known to the world.

You sit there still trying to figure out if this is a dream or not. You hear all the words, but they do not seem to be making sense until you hear the words, "I love you."

You blink your lovely eyes, once, twice, and a third time. My thoughts raced during that short time span. 'Did I misread something? Do you feel the same way?'

My heart started to sink in a bottomless pit of quicksand. A slow dreadful sink, to relive every detail, question everything I said and did to find out what I did wrong. What I said or did not say. No bottom to be able to pick myself up from. The burning pits of hell would be a vacation resort, compared to this type of agony.

Tears fall like tiny little stars from your eyes. You giggle and say, "I love you too, my lost American."

I do not know how to put into words how these three words made me feel. The falling sensation; still falling in love with you every second of the day, and at the same time soaring above the clouds.

I pull you in close to me. I kiss you again. I stand and offer you my hand, you take it, we go into the bedroom. You start to remove your clothes. I stop you and say, "I came back for you, not because of what we do, tonight let us hold each other."

You knew at that moment what true love was how it is supposed to feel like to receive if from a man that loves you more than anything in this world. This made you want me even more. You nod your head yes but continue to remove your clothes.

I cannot stop you. I stand there watching your clothes fall to the floor one by one. It was like watching a masterpiece being created right in front of my very own eyes.

I thought to myself, 'How unfair the advantages of that of women over men. A single look, a bat of an eye, a flick of the hand to brush your hair back, a smile, a touch, removing clothing...' My thought was broken.

You are in bed, and giggle, "Lost again."

A quick thought entered my mind in the old man's voice, 'It was the giggle.' I removed my clothes and climbed into bed.

We could not resist each other, nor the flames we fell through a night of love, compassion, intimacy, like no others on earth could experience. Everything pure, everything beautiful filled our minds, bodies, and souls.

We are laying on our backs when I turn to you and say, "I love you."

You smile and turn towards me and say, "Say it again, I love hearing you say it."

I repeated the words, "I love you."

You want to make a game out of it, "One more time?"

"I love you." I realized the game. "I love you; I love you; I love you."

You giggle and lean in and kiss me. You say in the sweetest voice and full of love, "I love you."

I lay back you place your head on my chest. You can hear my heart beating. You place your hand over your heart again both beating as one. You think, 'Connected.' You leave the 'somehow' off the thought because it is known, it is real, because we said it. We are connected by love.

You close your eyes, a gentle smile appears on your face as you feel yourself slipping into a perfect dream, all while in the arms of your true love.

True Love

We are on an afternoon walk, like we always do every afternoon. The day is perfect, not to warm but enough to need a shower after our walk. There is a light breeze that gives your hair life. Your hair rises and falls back into place, a graceful dance, each strand performing a perfect choreographed step in this dance routine.

The birds are chirping a song just for us. The only thing about this day that could go wrong is the dark cloud that is rolling in. But we do not let that stop us from enjoying the day, or the time that we get to spend together.

You are dressed in tight yoga pants, not because you like them, but you know they drive me crazy seeing you in them. You wore a sports bar flattering your perfect breast but not to revealing and that still drives me crazy. I will be honest everything in your closet drives me crazy. It just might be you.

I was wearing shorts that went down to just above the knees, and a water-wicking shirt. Nothing special. I still do not know what you see in me.

We are a block from our house, when you ask, "Did you feel that?" As you look up and raise your hand palm up to the height of your chest.

"No." But, as soon as I said the word, I felt the first rain drop.

You start to pick up the pace to get home.

"What's the hurry?" I ask in a teasing voice.

"It's about to storm." You reply.

I catch up with you and it starts. Large rain drops hitting everything, even the splashes of the drops are getting us wet. It is raining cats and dogs.

You start to run; I reach up and take your hand before you take the second step. We are only four houses away from our home. 'The rain is here we are already wet there is no need to run' I thought.

You turned looking at my hand holding yours. Then you look up, you see me smiling blinking the rain drops from my eyes.

I can see the shock in your eyes that I would stop you from getting home and out of this rainstorm that is crashing all around us.

Before you could say anything, I take a step closer to you, you can see it in my eyes. I see the rain flowing down your beautiful face, washing away all the shock or negative emotions away. Your body relaxes.

I reach in and kiss you; you kiss me back. We must have looked crazy to the outside world for doing this during a rainstorm. It feels like the rain is clearing our minds of what others may think and the outside world is gone.

The kiss ends slowly, you look into my eyes, you know that I want you. You feel the same sensation. You start to say something. I raise a finger to your lips. No words can do justice for what is happening at this very moment.

You must have agreed; your eyes look down and lick your lips. You take my finger into your mouth; you take your hands and hold my hand there in place.

Our eyes locked together, only blinking due to the rain. Each blink like that of a camera shutter snaps a picture of you. Storing what no professional photographer or camera could ever capture; perfection true and utterly perfect beauty. My mind has millions of these pictures of you stored away, and somehow your beauty grows more beautiful with each new one.

You remove my finger from your mouth, your amazing eyes become softer, the look I can never say no to. You smile, the smile that keeps my heart beating. I am yours, and nothing without you.

People say that their world falls apart after a divorce or breakup. I find them lucky they still have all the pieces. If anything, ever happened between you and I, I would have no world. I would be lost alone for all eternity. A punishment of living inside my own chest where my heart once was, it would be a cold empty space if you were not part of my life.

You take my hand in yours and we start to walk again, a little slower than our normal pace. We do not even notice the rain anymore; it has even washed itself from our minds. It is only you and I now.

Only through instincts do we end up at our front door. You pull out the key from your waist band, insert it and about to turn it; when I spin you around and lean into you. You are pushed up against the door. I kiss you passionately. My hands slide over your wet sports bra caressing your perfect breast.

You let out a small sigh you pull me in closer. With one hand you start to rub my crotch bringing him to life.

We must have looked like a couple of teenagers if anyone saw us. The horny teenage boy dropping off his date after a night out.

I wrap one arm around you and with the other I try the doorknob. Locked, I turned the key, and open the door, as it opened a crash of thunder sounds. It sounds like it is directly over us, it was so loud that we jumped at the sound. We both started to laugh, that nervous laugh.

You kiss me again and take a step backwards into the doorway. I follow in step.

Once inside and the door closed behind us. We pull each other close, nothing but the wet clothes are between us. We break and start pulling our clothes off. My wet t-shirt clings to my body, a small choir to remove it. You are having the same difficulties with the sports bra clinging to your soft skin due to the rain. I came in to help. You raise your arms. A pure look of trust is what you gave me. I lift your sports bra; you lower your arms once your head is clear.

Our shoes and socks are missing as we knew they could still be outside. Your hands are covering your breasts. I step in close I take your hands and remove them. My tongue dances tiny circles around your ever-hardening nipple, you pull me in close. I kiss, then take your nipple in between my teeth. I roll it gently, ever so light pressure. My tongue is moving in an up and down fashion on the very tip of your nipple.

You push me away from your breast, more clothing is stripped away. Your body a dream that only can live in the sleeping mind but is somehow standing fully nude in front of me. "What did I do to deserve a Goddess like you?" I asked

You smiled and said, "Everything."

Our naked bodies now with nothing to separate our skin to touch; you shiver. The air conditioning on our wet bodies started having effects that we did not notice before.

We move to the front room; I lay you down on the couch. I lay next to you and pull the throw blanket on top of us. I hold you tight and close, you can feel my body heat slowly warming your skin.

You reach down and take my cock in your hand. You bite down on my lower lip as if telling me not to move. I obey your unspoken command and kiss you.

My hand is lightly brushing up and down your stomach, starting from between your perfect breast down to just above your belly button. This sends tingles of pleasure up and down your spine. Your back arches off the couch just a fraction on each pass and let it fall again.

With each passing of my hand across your perfectly landscaped body, I allow my hand to travel a little lower. First past your belly button, next pass an inch lower, then another inch. Your breathing is becoming deeper with each pass that is moving further down. You know eventually where my hand will be, and you want it there now. You fight desperately the urge to grab my hand and place it where you want it. The anticipation is making you wet with desire. My hand touches your clit for a brief second then it is gone. You whimper, "No." You want it to stay there; you need it there.

You feel my hand making the next downward pass it is taking an eternity to make its way back to your sweet spot. Your breathing is getting faster; the tingles are more intense tracing up and down your spine. My fingertips find your clit slowly massaging tiny circles around it. You melt, no longer shivering from your rain-soaked skin and the cool air that has embraced it, but shivers from my gentle pleasurable touch. You want more; you need more.

You have brought my cock to life with your soft gentle strokes. As my hand traveled up and down your glorious body. You pull on my cock harder and harder wanting it, needing it inside of you.

My hand is still playing in your play ground; I kiss you deep and hard. I slowly slide one finger inside you. You break away from the kiss by turning your head to the side, you sigh with pleasure. With your head still to the side I take your ear lobe between my lips and kiss. I slowly move down and kiss your exposed neck. With your free hand you brush your still wet hair out of the way allowing my lips full contact on your soft silky skin.

My lips continue downwards to your collar bone, where I kiss gently one of the sensitive spots for you. Your head still to the side, you tilt it upwards to expose more of your lovely neck.

Your mind is clear only the pleasure matters.

You think, I wish that all days could be just as good as this. This man that is kind, treats me not just as a lady should be, but better if that is even possible. This man that truly cares, is intelligent, funny, and gives so much for nothing in return. This man that loves me, not for my body, looks or any of that, but for what he sees deep inside of me. You love me for the person that I am.'

My kisses bring you back to the moment. My lips are kissing the top of your breast now. You know where I am heading, and you want me there now, but you do not act on this impulse, this is beyond pleasure, this is true intimacy.

Your body amazes me each time I see, touch, and taste it. I am always nervous like it is our first time together. Always questioning myself, 'Do you enjoy this? Am I going too fast, too slow, too much, not enough?' I pray that you will say something if I was doing anything wrong. I only want to please you.

My kisses have reached your stomach. My lips miss a few due to your heavy breathing but are made up for by me placing my hand on your flat stomach and applying slight pressure.

My kisses are now at my hand that is playing. You sigh; you know that you will soon have your first orgasm. You want it. You start massaging your breasts with both hands. My first kiss sends intense pleasure through you. Your back arches, head rocks back, you inhale deeply and hold it in as if you can hold on to this sense of pleasure as long as you can hold your breath.

My tongue touches your clit. You exhale with a moan. Pleasure does not escape with your breath, it only intensified it. The pleasure increases with every touch of my hand, lips, and tongue. Your want has turned into need. You place your hands on the side of my head and start to pull my face close to your pussy.

You slowly start rotating your hips, you lift one leg and rest it on the back of the couch, the other leg is placed on my shoulder. Your inner thigh is caressing my cheek with your silky soft skin.

Your gyrating hips allows my tongue to find all your secret pleasure spots. When one is found you stop and let my tongue linger a second or two before you continue your hips on this magical merry-go-round of pleasure.

You gently pull my head from your pleasure spot; I kiss as you as you guide me upwards. Each kiss is like a spark of electricity running up and down your spin.

Some of these sparks collide, making your entire body tingle, the ones that crash together at the small of your back, makes you wetter. Your pussy craves my cock inside you. You want to feel it deep inside; you want the pleasure that it can only give you.

I kiss you deeply your juices still on my lips. You can taste your own sweetness.

My cock is rubbing against your playground. It runs from one toy to the next saving the best for last.

You are about to cum, you know the moment that I enter you, it will happen, you will not be able to control it. With that thought you reach down and slide my cock inside you.

Your head turns to the side; a pleasurable sigh escapes. Your eyes close. A gentle warm wave of pleasure washes over you. You can now feel a much larger wave approaching, one that could pull you out into this vast ocean and be lost forever. You could run from it and find safety, but you stay, damn it to hell.'

You think to yourself, lost in this sensation would be worth all of it.

You feel me entering slowly until my full length is inside of you. You sigh. I back out just as slow. You fight the urge to thrust your hips upwards so that I would be deep inside you again.

I increase my speed ever so slightly when I start my second stroke. You feel this larger, this dangerous wave approaching, inching its way closer and closer.

I start to vary the depth of which I enter you, first my full length, then just past the tip, next half my length of my cock. I am fighting with myself not to speed up and keep pushing myself all the way in with each thrust. This is not just for me, this is all about you. I want you to experience all the pleasure that I can give, and for as long as I can give it to you.

I keep up the variety of depth changing so nothing would become mundane, or predicable, because of this you cum on my cock on a long deep thrust. The dangerous wave looms over you ready to drag you away. You beg for it; need does not describe the strong desire you have for it. It has become like air, a thing that you must have to survive.

You say to me, "Cum inside me." In a winded whisper.

My thrust become full length again. Your eyes start to roll. You can see the wave falling almost on top of you. You can feel tiny drops of water land on your skin that sends tingles throughout your body as they land.

You moan loudly. I release my cum. The wave crashes upon you. You cannot move; you hold your breath.

A second shot of cum erupts inside of you. The wave pulls you out into the vast ocean. Your body starts to shake.

Another explosion fills you. You are out in the calm waters of the ocean now. Floating on your back. The entire world is gone. All worldly troubles, cares and worries vanish. You are at peace.

The last shot of cum deep inside of you. You exhale you start to sink. You do not have any fear. You allow your body to become one with this great ocean, one with all things, the bringer of life and death. You see all things are all connected; that happiness and sorrow are parts of the same.

You are at the point of understanding the meaning of life, when it all starts to fade. You cling for the answer, but it is out of your reach. You understand it was all an illusion produced by the intense pleasure and you smile knowing if any other person has ever experienced this that they are truly lucky and should never take anything or anyone for granted.

You are lying very still; breathing is slowing down to normal. I softly kiss you; you kiss me back. You wrap your arms around me. We lie there until your phone rings.

You sit up and reach for it, you look at the number and answer, "Hey sweetie what are you doing?" You say.

"Grandma! Can we come over this weekend if it is, ok?" One of our grandchildren asked."

Colombia

Chapter One: Trip to Colombia

My first book did much better than I ever thought it would. Writing in this genre with all the different types of fetishes and fantasies that are out there, I questioned myself. Since other books of this type carry the reader to a magical experience that they can picture as they read. I tried something different, something new I put the reader as a character, and it worked, again better than I ever imaged.

I also self-published my book in digital form and placed links to it everywhere I could, I was my own agent, so I had to self-promote as well, much harder than it sounds. The application I used allowed me to track the different languages the book was sold in and the countries that bought the book as well.

The first country on the list was America, second and very close to first place was England, might have a lot to do with that the main short story in that book that was named "England". What caught my eye was that Colombia was seventh of the top ten countries that bought my book.

The first book had a major theme that "I" was traveling for some reason or another to visit places that I wanted to relive the culture or live the culture that I was unable to do so while in the Navy. I thought if I wanted to write another book, I would need a reason to travel or come up with a new catch and it hit me; a book tour.

I wrote down the nine different countries names on separate pieces of paper, I left off the United States since I live here, and I can do this after I travel to the other countries. England, Germany, France, Finland, Sweden, Australia, Canada, Colombia, and Spain all folded up in little sheets of paper. I have been to four of the nine countries and cannot wait until I can go back and see more of these beautiful countries and visit the ones that I have not been to.

I placed the folded sheets of paper in a cup and shook them to ensure that they were mixed up and poured them all out on the desk. Nine and only one to pick. I reached down not even looking and chose one. I put it to the side and placed the other eight back in the cup for when I would return after the first trip. I looked down at the single folded piece of paper I could feel my heart beating faster, the excitement of traveling again.

I unfolded the paper and written upon it was the word 'Colombia'. I was excited that I have never been to South America before and the thing is I know nothing about the country. I jumped on my laptop and started searching everything that I could find out about the country. I went to government websites and travel reviews from people that have traveled there. I was satisfied that I was going to have a good time and get some work done promoting my book.

Now I needed to make some appointments and at first it was harder than I thought. I had to find a native Spanish speaking person to help with my phone calls to

schedule a book promotion in stores. My friend and I were able to secure three bookstores. We told them that we would call back in one week to confirm dates. I was not going to buy a plane ticket if I could not get into a store. The store managers were happy and looked forward to our call back.

Yes, the book was doing better than I thought but that does not mean that I have money to blow on first class plane tickets, so I searched online for the best prices and that meant waiting two months before I would be leaving. I also pulled up a map of the city and looked at where all the bookstores were located and found a nice hotel that would be in the center of all of them. I booked the hotel for six days. This would give me time to site see, write if I had the urge, and if needed work around a schedule mix up if one should arise.

A week later my friend and I hit the phones again to set dates and ask for the few things that I would require during the promotion. I do not think that I am a big-time writer that can demand things, but I would need a place to sit, a table, and I asked for two other things if the store could get a translator for me and two bottles of water. I was surprised at the willingness to help and they even offered food. I really felt like I was a superstar.

Chapter Two: Days 1 and 2 in Colombia

I arrive in Colombia after what seemed to be two years instead of two months. I was excited to be here and live in and experience this culture. I hailed a cab and handed the driver the address of the hotel.

I checked into the hotel and my room was better looking and more spacious than the pictures showed on the web-site. I walked back to the lobby and asked the concierge where I could find good local cuisine. He tells me in basic English that there is a small restaurant half a block from the hotel.

I ordered something that I will never be able to pronounce but it was some of the best food I have ever tasted. I walked back to the hotel.

My first promotion was scheduled for tomorrow. I checked everything that I brought, looked over the questions that I thought would be the most asked and thought about the answers that I would give. I pulled out my laptop I bought a power converter before I left and plugged it in. I started typing, not a second book, but notes on the trip just in case I could use some of it in a future book.

I woke up the next morning and I walked to the lobby and through it to the breakfast area. The amount of food available was enough to feed an army. I fixed myself a fruit bowl and a cup of coffee. I sat down in the empty area relaxing and enjoying the sweet flavors of the fruit and the earthy tones of the coffee. I was in no hurry and my appointment was not until later this afternoon. When setting the schedule, I wanted to make sure that most people would be out of school and off from work.

I finished and headed back to my room I did some more note taking and started to get ready.

I arrived an hour early at the bookstore. I introduced myself to the managers. They showed me to the back of the store where I would be set up. There was a table with two chairs, and in front of it were four rows of chairs with six in each row. I did not expect this.

I set my things down and started browsing the store. I knew that I would not find my book here, it is only in digit format at this time. I want to release it into paperback once it has been on the market for a year.

Fifteen minutes before the start time and the chairs are starting to fill up. I could see and hear the ladies whispering but could not make out a single word. A very attractive lady walks up to me. She holds out her hand and says, "I am your translator." She says in a Colombian accent but with perfect English. She gave me her name.

"Very nice to meet you." I say to her.

"I really enjoyed your book." She tells me.

I smile and say, "Thank you."

It is starting time; the managers of the bookstore stand in front of the table and thank everyone for showing up and if they have any question please be sure to ask, then they introduce me and the translator.

"Thank you all you lovely ladies for coming out today." I say to the crowd. I was not just saying this to please the crowd, they were all lovely. Colombian women are very beautiful.

Women are still showing up and now there is only standing room left.

The first question comes in and the translator asks for the lady, "Why do you write, with pronouns of I and you and such?"

I thank her for reading my book, and say, "I wanted my reader, you, to involve themselves in the story. The male character, when reading it can look like whatever you image, and you the reader, knows what they look like. That is why I do not describe what the characters physical appearances are."

The next question, "In your story "England" you have a detailed account of the female character did you base this character off a real person, have you met her?"

"At the time I wrote "England" I was talking with a lady from there. I asked a lot of question, and this gave me the idea of the female character. To answer your question more directly is yes, I based the character off of a real person, and sadly I have never met her."

"Are you working on another book?" The next question came in as I finished my answer.

"Honestly not at the moment but we will see, another idea or muse may enter my life and breathe life into another book." I answer and take a drink of water.

"I will be your muse." A lady shouted.

This brought laughter to the crowd and me. "Thank you, I just may take you up on the offer." I said, jokingly.

Three hours of questions went by fast, now an hour to sign autographs. The crowd formed a line and patiently waited their turn. I signed the back of my business card if they did not have anything for me to sign. The front of it had my name, email address, and link to buy my book that I set up after I published the book for fans to write to me.

I was surprised when a lady handed me a tiny sheet of paper folded up. I opened it and there was her phone number. I thanked her for it and signed a business card and gave it to her. I received ten more phone numbers. Each time it was like the first time asking a girl for her number and she giving it to you.

I helped the store employees clean up the area, they insisted that I did my part in helping with the increased business. They all thanked me and asked for my autograph even the males.

I turned to my translator and asked, "Where is a good place to get a drink and has good music?" I wanted to celebrate the first successful book promotion.

You told me that there is a place that is not too far from the bookstore that we were at, and said, "I cannot go since I will be at another book store tomorrow doing more translations for you."

I think you thought I was asking you out to get drinks. I guess it could have sounded like that, but I had no intentions of doing that. I did not say anything more about the subject but did say, "I will see you tomorrow." I did not know that you were hired for these translation jobs.

I went back to the hotel, ate dinner and started writing. I did not write in a book format but in note taking form. All the questions that were asked were just in case that I wrote a short story on this experience. I also made notes on the promotion on how the next one and any that follow could be better.

I then checked my email. This part of the job can get a little frustrating with all the pictures, half written stories, wanting to meet me, and the publishers that promise me the world. I am flattered by all the emails. My job is living in front of this laptop, and I cannot open pictures or follow links that people send, I could lose everything with one wrong email being opened. I answer the publishers with a pre-drafted email that thanks them for their offer but as of now I must decline.

When I pictured myself as a writer, I did not see myself answering emails, and posting updates on all the social media sites, but that is part of being a writer.

I looked down at the right bottom corner of my laptop and it was nine o'clock. If I wanted to go out, I better leave now. I jumped into a cab and told him where I wanted to go. He looked at me a little strangely and started heading there. I thought it was because I was an American.

Chapter 3: The Dance Club

I arrived at what I thought was going to be a bar, but instead it was a dance club. Me in my mid-forties almost turned around to go back to the hotel, but the voice in my head said, "You are already here."

I walked in and the place was larger than it looked from the outside. A section of seats, and one of the largest bars that I have ever seen, and I was in the Navy for twenty years, I have seen plenty of bars and clubs.

The crowd of people were all in their early to mid-twenties. I was the odd man out. What caught me off guard was that all these people were good looking.

I walk up to the bar and order a drink. I turned around and watched the sea of moving bodies on the dance floor.

One of the many things I wished that I would have learned in life is how to dance. Then a movement in the crowd caught my eye. Like a dorsal fin coming out of the water. I swear I saw it; the fear or excitement pumped through my body. Then it was gone just as fast or hidden in the waves of movement.

I start to scan the crowd more closely and I see the movement again. Hips moving in a circular motion and when at the point even with the shoulders, a very small barely noticeable pop or snap and the hips reverses the direction they were moving. It seemed to stop time this hypotonic rhythm. My eyes wanted to keep going around the mind had already made the pattern of the circle, but it was broken, my mind had to re-process what it just saw, causing a lapse of time.

My eyes followed this mesmerizing movement I could feel myself being put into a trance. I had to blink hard, or I would be sitting there drooling all over myself. I pull my eyes away from the intoxicant motion and look upwards. An angel of grace and beauty dancing.

You were dancing in the middle of the dance floor, keeping with the rhythm and beat of each song. When a guy approaches you to dance with you; you would either turn away from them or push them away. This was your time, your escape, your freedom from the world and you did not want any distractions.

I watch as you turn down advance after advance. I start to smile proud of you to hold your ground against the endless frenzy of sharks on the dance floor.

Your head turns in my direction, then your body turns to where now you are facing me. I swear that you are looking at me.

I feel a rush of excitement. I smile and then you smile then turn again. This feeling starts to fade, until you look over your shoulder and smile in my direction again.

The song ends, you have been out there since I arrived or at least I noticed the unpredictable movements. You walk off the dance floor to a group of friends. I watch you and you keep looking back over in my direction.

I turned back around to face the bar and ordered another drink. Still trying to process how the breaking of a pattern seemed to slow time. When I heard a voice behind me.

I could not understand what was said but the tone was not threatening, and the sound was like music to my ears. I turned around and you were standing there.

You say something in Spanish to me. I shake my head and say, "I'm sorry I don't speak Spanish."

You nod your head as if you understand then say, "American?"

"Yes." I said relieved that you understood me and that you could speak English.

"You watched me dance." You say.

"Yes, your moves, you dance amazingly graceful." I say testing your understanding of English.

Your eyebrows crinkle down, trying to translate what I just said. I then say, "You dance great."

"Thank you." You say smiling.

"Would you like a drink?" I ask.

"Please, thank you." You reply still smiling.

I let you order once you have your drink, we introduce each other and keep testing each other on our understanding of each other's language. Most of our communication was through body language, how we were facing each other, eye contact, posture, every little thing. Both of us were noticing every little detail.

You reach down and take my hand and lead me to the table where your two friends are sitting. You introduce me to them, and you start speaking Spanish.

I am trying to pick out words, but all foreign languages seem to be spoken at a speed of a thousand times faster than my native tongue. I try to pick out clues on the faces of these three ladies. Nothing stood out, or I could place.

A waitress came by we all ordered more drinks. A song comes on that you want to dance to. You look at me and reach out your hand. I held up my hands and said, "I can't dance." You looked upset and went out and started your hypnotizing moves once again.

One of your friends broke of my stare by asking, "what is it that you do?"

I love and hate that question. I am very proud and lucky that I am a writer and making a living from it, but when I tell someone the follow up question is always something like, what do you write about. Have I ever read anything that you have written?' Because of what I write most people find it taboo in day to day conversation but secretly love the content of the stories. It could also be that the town I live in is very small and mostly elderly people is why I have a hard time explaining this.

I answer honestly, "I am a writer."

"What do you write about?" The other one asked now seemed interested in the conversation.

I thought to myself, 'I'm here to meet fans and to promote my book so I might as well tell them.' "I write erotica, mostly short stories where two people run into each other, a chance encounter, and end up having sex."

They were either very intrigued, or they did not understand, or they thought that I was some type of pervert. But, for the people that have read my book knows what they are about and not some crazy fetishes filled book or story. I am not saying that there is anything wrong with that either, but it is not my writing style.

You come back and drink your drink and head to the bar by yourself. I watch you. I feel that you are giving me the cold shoulder because I cannot dance and talking with your friends.

You came back and you brought me a beer. I thank you. You sit down, and your friends start talking in the hyper speed of Spanish to you. I could only assume that they were telling you what I just told them. You look up at me and smile and say, "Sex writer."

"Yes and no." I say embarrassed.

"Tell me." You say.

I do my best to describe that I try to capture what the lady in the story may feel and see in her mind during sex. The excitement the pleasure and awakening of the senses during a pleasurable moment.

You nod your head in understanding, but I can see that you do not understand everything.

You understand more than you are letting me believe. Your emotions are on a high from dancing, you feel good, sexy, and wanted when you are on the dance floor. The talk about sex and how these feelings are intensified in how I describe it is causing those feelings to grow stronger, and they are directed towards me.

Another song you like comes on and you stand up and head out to the dance floor. I cannot keep my eyes off of you. A shark circles and comes in close; you turn him away with a stiff arm to his chest. You look back to where I am sitting, and you smile. This smile draws me into your seductive dance. Another shark approaches from behind, you do not turn him down. You push are rub your perfect ass against him while you are looking at me still smiling. You lick your lips. Your mind flashes a vision of me dancing behind you and you want me.

I stand up and walk out into the dance floor. I see your eyes brighten. I stand in front of you not moving just standing there watching you. You place your hands on my chest and slowly move in close moving away from the guy behind you. Your hands move to my shoulders, and you press your body up against mine. I can feel your breast against my chest, so firm.

You slide your hands down to my waist and push them to my side to sway with the music. You lock your eyes on mine and mine to yours.

My hands move up to your face and rest on your cheeks then slowly slide down to the side of your neck then your shoulders.

You spin around your perfect ass is pushed up against me. You look back at me and smile you reach behind you and place your hands on my waist again to guide me.

You arch your back as you lean down. I place my hands on the small of your back and slide them upwards until they reach your shoulders.

I could not believe that I was out on the dance floor and dancing. Dancing with a beautiful lady. The experience was intoxicating.

The song ends, and you take my hand and lead us back to the table. One of your friends had left and the other looked like she wanted to leave. You two talk. It seemed that she wanted you to leave with her, but you refused.

Once your friend left, I told you, "It is getting late, and I needed to get back to my hotel."

"One more drink and one more dance, then we go." You said.

I could tell that you were getting drunk, but I walked to the bar and ordered you another drink. When I turned around you were standing there. "Thank you." You said as I handed you the drink. You drink it down.

"We go now." You say.

"What about your dance?" I asked.

"Same song as before." You say as you take my hand and lead us out of the club. Once out you ask, "Where you stay at?"

You start to lead us down the street. I ask, "Do you want to take a cab?"

"Not far of a walk." You say.

We are at my hotel and walk in. We walked through the lobby to get to my room. I am standing in front of the door, and I look behind me you are standing next to the jacuzzi. I walk over to you.

You turn and grab me by my arms and with strength that should not be possible from such a small frame pulls and spins me towards the water.

I feel gravity taking its hold and I reach and take hold of your wrists and pull you in with me. A loud splash echoes into the swimming area as we both land in the warm water.

You are pressed up against me. We look at each other and we kiss. The water's temperature seems to rise with the kiss. We break the kiss you pull your wet shirt off. A silk lacy white bra; see through because of the water. The lace clings to your perfect breasts, your nipples poking at the fabric trying to escape.

My shirt comes off and back into each other's arms kissing again. A deep passionate kiss. I can feel your hands working on my pants. They are soaked, making them difficult to remove.

I pull away from the kiss and start to remove my pants. I notice that my shoes are still on, I remove them while still trying to remove my pants. You take off your shoes.

My wet clothes are in a pile of wet mess at the side of the jacuzzi along with yours.

I pull you in close again my hands slide down your perfect body down to your waist. I undo the button of your black shorts I pull down slowly and as I do I kiss your neck, your breasts and stomach. You step out of your shorts. I see silky white panties. The water has turned them see through and clings to your soft skin. You ask, "You like?"

"I do." I answer.

You think to yourself, 'I like this man he is different from all the others that live here.' You pull me in close to you and kiss me.

You reach behind you and unclasp your bra; you slide your arms out of the straps. The cups of the bra cling to your wet skin.

You reach down and find my cock and start to stoke up and down. I remove my underwear.

I peel off your bra. My mouth takes one of your nipples, my tongue plays with your hard nipple. My hands side down your sides to find the thin straps of your panties and slowly push them down.

You hold my head in place while my tongues dances. You picture you and I are on the dance floor dancing a very seductive dance.

You lean up against the edge of the jacuzzi placing your elbows on the sides to give yourself support. You let your body float to the surface of the water.

I pull your panties the rest of the way off, I bend down and move in close to your wanting pussy.

You look down at me, the anticipation of me and my tongue on your pussy is making you wet with lust. Your hands are caressing your breasts. You pull one close to your mouth, and you lick your own nipple.

My tongue finds your clit, the dance begins. You are back on the dance floor; all the other people fade from your sight. You can hear the music, you can feel the music deep inside you, but you cannot move. You try with all your might, but something is holding you. You feel the music building inside of you. You know what the cause of this paralysis is, pleasure. You begin to shake; you hear your own moans of pleasure over the music from within. You cum hard and fast, and you want more.

You push yourself from the edge pushing me along with the movement. Your body splashes into the water tiny waves are set over the edge. The walk area around the jacuzzi is getting wet as well.

You stand your perfect body standing half out of the warm water, beads of water trickle down. You push back your hair to remove it from your beautiful face.

You turn and move to the edge you lean over the edge; I move in behind you. You look back at me and smile, then say something in Spanish that I do not understand.

I play with your pussy and clit with my cock, teasing you. You push your hips against me trying to force my cock inside you.

The dance floor appears in your mind again. I am standing a few feet away from you, facing you. The music is just starting. You stand there while I start moving towards you. My steps shuffle with the rhythm, my hips move to the beat, my arms move with the notes floating around you. You have never seen such graceful dance moves, alluring movements a dance of seduction that is driving you to want me even more.

I reach and grab a handful of your wet hair, I pull, and your head is pulled upwards at the same time I thrust my cock deep inside of you. A loud moan escapes your lips. You inhale a deep breath as I retract my cock half the length and thrust again. You start rocking your hips and pushing yourself against me.

You are still unable to move on this dance floor in your mind. My body is moving closer and closer to yours. My movements are like a spell being cast over you. My body is so close to yours you can feel my body heat on your skin. My hand moves towards your lovely face and traces the outlines without touching.

You feel the onset of your second orgasm you try to slow it; you want more you want this pleasure to last but the pleasure is too great.

My pace is steady however my thrusts vary all while your hips keep pushing harder and harder.

The song is almost over you feel your body getting weak. You just want to let go. I have circled your body and even when I was at your back you knew exactly where I was, from the warmth radiating from me.

The last note sounds the music stops. Your knees buckle you fall. I am there and catch you. The pleasure of my touch releases a rush of excitement your body shakes in my arms.

You push hard, my cock deep inside your wet pussy. You cum. Your body shakes your back arches. Your eyes roll upwards. Your breathing is shallow quick inhales and exhales. Your hands are grasping for anything to hold on to.

Your body relaxes I pull myself out of your tight pussy. Your hips drop slightly. I put the tip of my cock on your tight little asshole.

You look back, you do not say anything, but your eyes and smile tell me you want it. I slowly push the tip in. Your eyes go wide, your head tilts downwards you exhale deeply.

I push half of my cock inside your perfect ass and slowly pull out. Then push inwards again.

The most seductive Latin song starts playing while I am still holding you on the dance floor. I help you to your feet. We are both nude. There are no feelings of embarrassment or shame. It seems that we are works of art the dance floor a canvas, and the music is our muse, to create a masterpiece. The notes become the palette from which we will work, our bodies the brushes.

My cock is fully inside you; you sigh my thrusts have not increased in speed. You start moving your hips to the music inside your mind, you are now in control of everything.

Our bodies move with angelic like grace on the dance floor, our footsteps leaving trails of paint, yours bright red, mine a bright blue. This dance a mix of ballet, Salas, vernacular, and tango, with each seamless style change the colors change.

The song is purely instrumental with each note played it finds a place inside of you that brings pleasure and an understanding of what everything means.

Your hips are moving faster and faster. Water is slashing out of the jacuzzi, the sound of our bodies slapping together mixed with your moans were becoming louder. We were to caught up in the moment to care if anyone could hear or see us.

You disassociate with your dancing body for a brief second. You are looking down upon yourself and me dancing, you see the paint that our bodies were leaving on the dance floor. The image was breathtaking, never have you seen such beauty. You name it, 'Baile de Sexo'. You re-enter your body as the song is about to end.

My cock erupts it first shot of cum in your ass. You feel the warmth, you cum at the same time. You wish this 'Dance of Sex' could last.

The song is on its last notes, but the tone is loud, you jump towards me flattening yourself while in the air while doing a half twist. Pure trust, pure faith is all you have now.

I thrust my cock deeper inside your tight ass and release another seed. Your body goes relaxed for a brief second.

My arms wrap around your body safely, bringing you towards me. The last note is struck. All the pleasure that was built up is released throughout your body.

You cum again you never have had multiple orgasms so quickly together. Your body shakes and again your knees go weak. You are breathing heavily. You are speaking in Spanish again. I can from the tone and volume of your voice that it is not of anger but that of pleasure.

I help you out of the jacuzzi I gather the wet clothing, and you follow me into my room.

We both walk into the bathroom I hang the wet clothes on the shower curtain rod. You turn on the shower and ask, "Shower with me?"

I woke up the next morning and you are not there.

Chapter Four: Day Three A Story Come True

I woke up and thought to myself, 'What a dream. So real, and life like.' My eyes open, and I am the only one in the hotel bed. I head to the bathroom, and I see the clothes I was wearing last night still hanging up on the shower curtain rod. Your clothes are gone.

I am getting ready for the day. I open my laptop and start writing everything I could remember last night. I lose track of time. My alarm goes off letting me know that I must get ready for the next bookstore.

The owner and managers are excited to see me. The table and the rows of chairs where place more in front of the store.

I set up my things at the table and I wanted to check the sales of the book. I looked over all sales and they were still climbing, then checked Colombia, and it was still seventh, but the number was very close in taking over sixth place. The book tour is working better than I would have ever guessed.

My translator walks up to me and said, "How are you today?"

"I am good, thank you and yourself?" I asked.

Fifteen minutes before the start of the onslaught of questions and the sexual tension so thick I could cut it with a knife from all these ladies in the crowd. The size of the crowd is easily double the size of the first.

Start time and again most of the questions were the same as the first, which I excepted. The most common were, "Was any of it real?" Are you writing another book? Where do you draw from for inspiration?" Then a question that myself did not know the answer to hit me.

"How is it that when the female character, looks inside herself during the act or before and even afterwards, that you are able to describe what a lot of women think and feel during these times?" My translator said.

My first response that I thought of was, 'I do not know.' But that would not be true, I wrote it, so I must have some idea or think that I do.

I responded, "To be honest I have never really thought about it, until you asked the question. When I am writing about the act of sex, sure I can describe the physical act and that would attract some readers, but I wanted something more than a taboo, raunchy story. I wanted my readers to feel the emotions, not just the pleasures of sex. I wanted to go deeper into the mind, almost into the subconscious and paint a true picture of what I think a lady would feel during the act of sex." I take a drink of water. "That is why I use something like fire, falling or a tidal wave, we all know that they can be very dangerous, just like sex can be, but in the story, I take away the danger and replace it with pleasure, extreme pleasure just like sex." I answer.

When the translator finished talking. I looked out into the crowd. I could literally see all these ladies melt. What have I done and what did I create with my book?

The line formed for me to start signing, the managers were rushing them along, I was already two hours over schedule. I was looking down reaching for another business card, and a new pen out of my bag, when the last lady stepped up to the table.

"You can make it out to..." A lovely British accent reaches my ears.

I looked up my mind flashed to the entire story of 'England'. It could not be the lady that pushed me to publish my stories, that is impossible and why would she be in Colombia. My story painted the perfect Goddess, an angel of pure, true beauty and somehow my words, my thoughts, my imagination created this lady that is standing in front of me.

"Are you from 'England'?" I asked if you were from the story, not from the country, but I knew what you thought when I asked.

A sheepish smile filled your lovely face, "Yes I am." You said.

I felt lost like the male character in 'England' my mind raced, and I finally asked, "I hope that you did not come all the way from England to meet me, I am planning a trip there?"

"Oh! No, I am here on my studies, and I heard that you would be in town. I wanted to meet the man behind the words that are driving all the women in England crazy." You say with a smile.

"What do you mean driving the women crazy?" I ask.

"It must be the different culture, we want a man that is like that in your stories, a real man, a kind and gentle man. You stripped away the playboy billionaire to a regular man that could be just around the corner, or half a world away and that is what the woman in England talk about." You tell me.

I then realized what The Beatles must have felt like when they toured America, a fan base of mass women just wanting to see them, to hear them, dare I say be with them. The thought quickly faded they do not want to be with me, but they want the male character in my stories.

"I need to clean up here really quick, but if you do not mind would you stay, and we can talk some more?" I asked.

"That would be lovely." You said with a smile.

My mind flashed again to the story of 'England' was she quoting the female character, or did you really mean it.

I packed up my things and talked and thanked the owner and managers for their hospitality and returned to where you were patiently waiting.

"Would you like to go and get tea or coffee?" I suggest.

"That sounds wonderful." You say in that beautiful, sweet English accent.

We walk to a coffee shop, the man behind the counter greets us in Spanish. You greet him back.

I was not really surprised that you spoke Spanish you did say that you were here for your studies, but I asked, "You speak Spanish?"

"You don't?" You asked.

I laugh, "You know that I don't I had to use a translator." I reply.

You smile and say, "What would you like, I will order if you find us a place to sit?"

You come back with my coffee, and you have an Earl Grey tea. I ask, "You said that you are here for your studies what are you studying?"

"My field of study is Archeology; I am writing my thesis or dissertation on how ancient civilizations and their cultures still have an impact on today's society. I know it sounds crazy, but they left so much, and we really know so little of them, but they still left so many things that we still do in day-to-day life that there has to be a connection." You tell me with passion in your voice.

I am hooked on every word. I say, "I find this extremely fascinating that ancient civilizations still have impacts on society and I do not think it is crazy."

"Why do you find it fascinating?" You ask and look at me with questioning eyes.

"I am a writer, and I have a natural curiosity about things that I do not know or understand and who knows I may be able to use some of the knowledge gained in an upcoming book." I let you know with a smile.

"Your beautiful eyes light up and smile, "There is another book coming out?" You ask with excitement.

"I have not started another book, but that does not mean that some idea will not strike me." I answer not to promise anything but keep the possibility open.

"I really do think you should, they are uniquely written and very..." You stop yourself not embarrassing yourself.

I smile knowing how hard it is to talk about sex in front of a stranger. It is a taboo subject that society has told us that it is a stay away subject, just like politics, and religion. I say. "Can you tell me more about your research, I promise I will not give anything away until after you turn in your dissertation and I will reference it to ensure that you receive all the credit for your work."

You start to think about it, you place yourself in your home back in England sometime after you have finished your studies, and you smile to yourself. You can feel yourself sitting in your bed. You can feel the book in your hands you can tell the weight of it. You are aware of your breathing, slow inhales and exhales. You can hear the crisp new pages rubbing together as you turn the page of this new erotica book. The aroma of a new book, the paper, the ink fills you with slight pleasure and anticipation of what lays ahead on the next page. You have a glass of wine on the night stand the sweet taste of the grapes and flowery notes dance across your lips and tongue. A small candle mixes with the scent of the book, a sweet vanilla flavor that you can almost taste that enhances the flavor of the wine. A perfect night, to relax and enjoy a book.

You are devouring every word; each word hypnotizes you into feeling all the pleasures as if you are the character in the story.

You can feel the soft silk of your nighty lightly resting on your skin. You start to caress your breast over the silky fabric with your free hand. Your hand jumps up to turn the page. Then return slowly your fingers circle your nipple. Your breathing becomes deep and slower.

Your hand moves lower applying slight pressure as it moves over your flat stomach. Your reading slows as you feel yourself becoming the character in the story. Your hand moves further down and finds your secret spot. Your stomach jumps with the first touch. Your eyes close for a few seconds, your lips part, your tongue licks them and another deep breath through your parted lips.

Your eyes open, a quick refocus and you continue to read, with cat like reflexes your hand is up turning the page and returns to what you were doing just as fast. The story is describing the pleasure of the act of sex between two strangers that cannot control themselves. Your hand moves faster rubbing your clit faster and faster wanting the described pleasure to magically transfer from words to physical pleasure.

The book falls from your hand. You are unable to stop what you are doing. You sit up and pull the nighty up and over your hand, you raise your hips and remove your silky panties and throw them to the floor. You lay down and start again, just as fast as you had been before you removed your clothing. You lose control, your hips come off the bed as you play. You moan, breathing fast, eyes closed. Your fingers of one hand massaging your clit, the other hand allows two fingers to slide inside of you. You exhale fully. Your back slightly curls as your fingers enter your tight wet pussy. You pull your fingers halfway out and push back in, your back arches, bringing your hips off the bed again.

You increase the speed of which your fingers are giving you pleasure, your hips moving up and down and side to side. Your moans are increasing your own pleasure. All is forgotten except for the pleasure that you are giving yourself. You let yourself go, you feel the rush, you cum. You stop all movement of your fingers. Your legs come together squeezing your hands, your back is pushed into the bed, your head tilted up and to the side and uncontrollable tremors consume your body. Your breathing is quick trying to catch it as if it had escaped. You stay that way for five seconds until your legs relax, you remove your fingers from your wet pussy, while you slowly and gently rub up and down on your clit. Deep breaths, shaking, you want to continue but the pleasure has overwhelmed all your senses.

You lay there until you notice the book resting next to you. You pick it back up and look at the page that you were on. There you see what sparked all of excitement, your name and the work that I referenced for the part of this story in an erotica fantasy, as well as you are being portrayed as the female character.

I am sitting across the table from you, and I notice that you are shifting in your seat, and your breathing is erratic, your eyes become softer, and your blinking slows.

Suddenly you sit straight up in your seat. A surprised look of confusion and embarrassment fills your face. Your posture changes from being relaxed and calm to that of acute awareness and uncomfortableness.

"Will you please excuse me; I need to go to the ladies room." You say as you stand and walk towards the restrooms.

I thought that I may have pushed to hard asking about your research. Then, replaying the events of the last few seconds I realized what had happened.

You return a short time later. "I understand that if you do not want me to use any or part of your research. I have to be careful of what I say when I talk about what I am writing for the fear that someone may take an idea and run with it." I say.

"Oh! No that is not it, it is no one has shown interest in my work except you and my professor. Even the under graduates do not think there is any correlation between them and us." You tell me.

You continue with a recent find and you want me to see the discovery if I am able. I could see the fascination that this find had on you.

The way you described the similarities made perfect sense, granted with technologic advances it could be difficult to put the pieces together, but there was a very thin faint line that was connecting us with them.

Your phone goes off. "I am sorry, but I need to leave. I have a meet that I must attend." You say with disappointment in your voice. "How long are you going to be touring in Colombia?" You ask.

"I will be here for another three days. I do not have anything tomorrow I planned on seeing some of the sites, day after that another bookstore, then return home in the evening of the third day. May I ask why?" I ask you.

"I would like to show you something that I think will peek your interest, and I really enjoyed talking with you. I will meet you at the bookstore day after tomorrow if that is alright?" You ask with excitement in your voice.

"I look forward to our next time we get the chance to talk." I say as I stand. "It was a pleasure to get to know you and an honor to speak with such an intelligent beautiful lady as yourself."

You start to blush and look down at the floor. "Thank you, I will see you day after tomorrow." You turn and walk towards the exit of the shop.

I stand there watching this angel walk away. Was this the feeling that I was trying to describe, of the female character, when the male character walked towards the custom's booth? The feeling of a connection being broken because of some obligation that one thinks that must be fulfilled.

You turn and smile and wave as you push the door open as you leave. I felt the connection reestablished; this new feeling was nothing like what was implied as in the walk away paragraph. This feeling of finding something verses the feeling of losing something.

I sat back down and pulled out my laptop. I started writing. I let the feelings of this excitement guide my fingers over the keys. I was not even thinking of what I was typing. I was there for another two hours and two more cups of coffee.

I went back to the hotel. I set everything up on the desk. I wanted to continue writing but I was getting tired, so I removed my shoes and laid down on the bed.

I closed my eyes for what seemed like a minute when I heard a knock on the door.

I opened the door thinking that it would be someone from the hotel. Instead, there was a little package wrapped in brown paper. I took it inside and opened it. A handwritten note was on top of the freshly washed and folded clothes. It read: I borrowed these clothes when I left early in the morning. They are washed.

Chapter Five: Day Four Interview

I woke up to a knock at the door. My eyes open and I think to myself, 'Who could this be?'

Another knock on the door. I get up to answer the door. I look through the peep hole. I saw that the translator was standing there.

I open the door. I looked at her, "What are you doing here?" I ask.

"A reporter contacted the bookstores wanting to do an interview, which they then turned the reporter to me, and that is why I am here." You said.

"How did you know what room I was in." I ask as I open the door wider.

You walk in and say, "I told the front desk that I am your translator, and that I said that you were a writer and it was important that I speak to you in person."

I thought that this would never have in the United States, but this is Colombia. "Please sit. When will this interview take place?" I ask, as you sit at the desk.

"I will call them and meet us wherever we say, but it has to be done within the next two hours if that is alright with you?" You let me know the details.

"Sure, that will be fine, let me get ready really quick." I tell you.

You stand and say, "I will wait in the lobby." You walk out of the room. I jump in the shower, shave, brush my teeth and get dressed.

I walk out to the lobby you are sitting there with a magazine in your hands reading. "Are you ready?" I asked.

You stand, and we walk out of the hotel. We took a cab to a little bar, that was twenty minutes from the hotel.

The bar was quiet and dark, I ordered a bottle of water and sat at a little table. Ten minutes went by and the reporter walked in. He waved and walked towards the table.

We introduce ourselves and the interview starts. My first interview. The questions were mostly the same as what all the ladies had asked, so nothing made me have to really think of the answers. Then I asked a question that I liked.

"While you are describing the act of sex, you leave the sense of time out of it, you jump from the physical to the psychology or thoughts of the female character, so the sex seems to take very little time, could you explain why you did this?"

I smiled, and clear thoughts rushed in, and I told him, "What would a reader think if I wrote something like 'I looked at my watch and it was one: thirty-two and we started and looked at it again and it was four: fourteen when we finished." I had a drink.

He understood but made a statement. "But the acts seem so short in time wise."

"Time is what we think it is.   Yes, it is a measurement, but it is also the perception of an experience how time seems to slow or speed up given a person's emotional state, but I tried to leave subtle hints in some of the stories that a reasonable time has elapsed." I try to explain my beliefs about how time works and of how the mind works.

The interview lasted about an hour. He thanked me for my time and told us that the article will be sent to my publisher's address. I smiled and thought 'I would have to get it translated, but I would have an article in a publication.'

I went back to the hotel and laid down. So much for sightseeing.

Chapter Six: Day five Discovery

I woke up and I felt refreshed and a little excited the last bookstore on this little tour, and the seeing of the British Student afterwards. I could not contain myself. I had plenty of time and I was ready within thirty minutes. I went to the bookstore three hours early.

The biggest one of them all that I have toured here. I was thankful that they had a coffee shop built in to the store. I set up my laptop and started brainstorming.

"Excuse me, may I sit with you?" The lovely accent reached my ears.

I turned, and my eyes saw perfection. I stand and say, "Please."

There was about an hour until the start of the questions and answers. We sat there and talk the feeling of being connected was still there.

"Are you going to stay for the questions and answers?" I ask.

"Of course, and if you are not busy afterwards, we could go get something to eat?" You say with a shy smile.

The gathering of ladies outnumbered the first two bookstores. I did not think that these many ladies would show up for a book signing when there was not a book to sign.

The questions came, and I gave the answers the best that I could. No real new questions. I was paying more attention to you even though you did not ask a question. I was sneaking glances at my phone to keep the time and when there were thirty minutes left, I had the translator inform the ladies that I would start signing and meet them one by one.

The last lady in line and I signed the back of my business card. She kissed the writing and held it to her chest smiling as she turned and walked away. I could not help but think that I made her day. I started packing up my things while you sat there with your laptop typing away.

I thanked the managers for the opportunity that their store offered for me. They thanked me for choosing their store.

We walked out of the bookstore. "I know a little place would you like to try it? It is where I have eaten every night and even though I cannot pronounce anything on the menu everything is delicious that I have tried?" I asked.

"I love trying new places and things." You tell me.

We arrive at the restaurant and take a seat in the back so that we can talk. "This is what I wanted to show you." You say as you pull out your laptop. You press a few keys, then turn it around so that I can see the screen.

At first, I did not know what I was looking at. It seemed to be a slab of stone with engravings on it. The first picture showed the length of the slab which was about six feet long, but not all one piece there were parts that were missing but it was pieced together like a puzzle.

The second picture was a top looking down on this discovery and still I was unsure why you wanted me to see this. The third picture revealed the reason why. The following pictures were close ups so that I was able to see them. It showed block like figures carved into the stone. It was a story out of art.

The story was that of a man and a woman. It was easy to tell due to the penis like engraving protruding from where the waist and legs meet and the breasts like shapes located on the chest area on a different figure. The gest of this ancient story was a man walks up to a woman and mingles then has sex.

"How old is this?" I ask.

"600 to 1600 CE." You said with a large smile. You could see that I was totally in awe of what you were showing me.

"This culture was depicting or writing about sex. I do not if it was for education or arousal or really anything, but it does show that they wanted to capture the act and let others see. Almost like I try to do with my writing. This is truly amazing." I tell you as I look over the display. I can see your beautiful smiling face. I returned the smile.

"Please you cannot tell anyone about this, until after my research and all the red tape of governmental control has passed." You tell me, with the slightest flicker of doubt, that you should not have shown me this.

"I promise that I will wait until I hear from you to act upon anything that I see here." I assure you. I close the laptop and slide it back to you. You smile with relief and a deep exhale. "Thank you for trusting me with this it means the world to me."

"I do not know why I showed you. It could be that you are a writer and would appreciate such a find and not look at it as some would consider distasteful but see it as it truly is; art and beauty." You confess.

We continue talking about the find, and how it could relate to the modern world. The conversation turns towards my work as a writer, then leads into each other's personal lives. I cannot recall the last time that I had such a stimulating and enjoyable conversation. I started to feel like you have been part of my life, for much longer than this little meeting, an intense connection that I have never felt before.

I pay for our meals and continue to talk. You think the same as I that you feel that we are reconnecting from childhood, a playmate that moved away but now brought back into your life filled with wonderous stories and adventures that you want to be part of. Or is it that you want to be part of the next book?

We walked out of the restaurant and just started walking. We walk towards the hotel that I am staying at, once in front of it. "I would really enjoy continuing our conversation, we can place our things in my room then head to the bar?" I ask.

I can see the hesitation. "One drink and conversation is all I am asking." I say in a calming voice.

"O.K., one drink." You allow yourself to be guided.

We drop our things off in the room and head to the hotel bar. You order a glass of wine, and I order a beer. We sit at the bar facing each other and keep diving into each other's personal life and past trying to learn what each other likes, dislikes, hopes, and dreams.

You finish your glass of wine at the same time I finish my beer. You turn to the bartender and order another glass of wine, "Would you like another?" You smile at me.

I playfully reply, "Are you trying to get me drunk?"

You laugh and order the beer. Once the drinks are handed to you. You stand up and take my hand and lead us to a small little couch away from the bar. We sit and have a more playful and flirtatious banter with one another. I reach over and take your hand in my and pull it up to inspect it.

"What are you doing?" You ask with a smile on your face.

"Such beautiful hands for a lady that plays in the dirt all day." I say with a smile. "Really I just wanted to hold your hand." I let you know.

You do not pull your hand away, as I lower it from my inspecting eyes. I let both of our hands rest on my leg as we keep the push and pull of attraction going.

We are there on the couch for about twenty minutes. I stand and offer my hand. You reach up and take it. I help you stand. "Where are we going?" You ask.

"To get a drink to go, then my room. I would like to show you what I have been working on if I can trust you?" I say.

I order the drinks and head to my room. Once inside I open my laptop and pull up my brainstorming notes and let you sit down to read what is there.

While you are reading, I place my hands on your shoulders and slowly and gently start massaging your shoulders. Your head slowly moves side to side allowing my fingers and thumbs to apply pressure at the base of your neck. Your lips part you lick your lips. You want more than my hands on your shoulders and neck.

"That feels so good, please don't stop." You said.

I continue with your shoulders for a few more minutes. I can see that you have not scrolled down to the next page of my notes. You are lost in the pleasure of the massage. My hands move forward from your shoulders and down to your collar bone. I gently rub; I do not feel any resistance from you. I move my hands further down, as I lean down and kiss your neck. No resistance.

I move one hand further down and towards the center of your chest, the other hand follows. I circle your breasts without touching them and move my hands back to your shoulders. I can feel that your breathing is deeper than normal.

You stand and turn to face me you lean in and kiss me. I embrace you and take a small step back you take a step forward, another step back you follow. I reach the edge of the bed and let myself fall backwards while bringing you down with me.

We kiss as we start removing our clothing your beautiful body naked on top of mine.

My hands run down your side and take your hips firmly and pull them up. You feel my stiff cock rub up against your clit sending a tingle of electricity through your body. You feel yourself getting wet and wanting my cock inside you.

You slide your hips forward and back. My cock teasing your clit with each pass.

You find yourself in an open field with soft grass underneath your bear feet. The perfect temperature. Lush green grass as far as the eye can see in all directions. You raise your head to the sky with your eyes closed. Allowing the calm and peace fills your very core.

You raise your hips as you reach down and take my cock to guide it into your tight pussy. You slowly lower yourself until my full length is inside of you. Your head tilts upwards and you stay there a few seconds.

You raise your hips and lower them with each cycle you increase speed. I begin to match your movements with my own thrusts.

You open your eyes, and you can see storm clouds above you. Dark ominous clouds. Lightning strikes a hundred meters away; you can feel the power and the charge of electricity enter your body.

You feel the pleasure growing wanting to escape tingling sensations radiate throughout your body. You let yourself flow with these sensations; you let yourself cum on my cock deep inside you.

Lightning is striking the ground all around you moving closer and closer. You do not try to run. With each strike that moves closer the power increases and the pleasure increases. You have never felt this much pleasure before.

I roll you over; I kiss you as I enter you. You bite my lip. I thrust deep inside. You let out a sigh and turn your head to the side. I reach down and kiss your neck. You push your hips up and towards me to ensure each thrust is deep inside of you.

The last strike only a meter away. Your eyes only see pure white, calm, peace, and safety, nothing will harm you. The electric charge races through your entire body, you are aware of every cell in your body. Each vibrating with pure pleasure.

You feel a powerful energy building inside you deep from inside your core. You picture it as a small electric blue ball of light, growing. Small electric sparks jump and arch across the surface of this beautiful ball. Some of these sparks fly off and hit your pleasure centers throughout your body. You feel that you will be overloaded with pleasure.

My hips thrust hard and my shaft slides deep as it spills the first seed deep inside you.

The attraction of power from your core sends up a flash of pure energy as the bolt of pure power crashes down, your entire body shakes and trembles.

Your legs wrap around me squeezing tight. Your hips rise off the bed keeping me deep inside you. Your eyes roll as your head tilts upwards. A long moan escapes your parted lips.

The sound of thunderclaps above you, a long rolling sound. You can feel the vibrations of the sound wash over you, the sound was not frightening but calming smoothing wrapping you in an invisible blanket.

Your hips lower but your legs are still tightly wrapped around me, I retract an inch and push again another shot of cum fills you.

The storm is passing yet lightning still strikes behind you small jolts of pleasure still reach the core of your being. Sending uncontrollable spasms coursing through your body.

Your legs loosen there hold; I retract half the length of my cock and push in again an explosion of cum in 0your wet pussy.

You fall to the soft grass as the dark storm cloud moves out of your sight. The sky clearing becoming clear peaceful blue that refreshes your thoughts. You feel a light breeze brush across your naked body; you breathe in this breeze with the scent of purity which calms you even more. You close your eyes.

I slide out of you and move next to you. Your eyes are closed; your breathing is returning to normal. You turn to face me, you smile and say as you open your angel eyes, "You will have to let me know when you are touring England."

I Am

I am all things of the matter of the heart
I have been and will continue to be used
As inspiration or as a muse
For I am
Strong yet fragile
Beautiful yet ugly
I have made appearances in all types of works
The greatest tragic love story some may say I had
my part
For I am
Love and sadness
Life and death
I am everyday common people
Elevated to royalty amongst my peers
For I am
Sweet but bitter
Pleasure and pain
I may or may not be your favorite
Yet you cannot forget me
For I am
Soft yet hard
Sorrow and joy
I can be there at birth and at death
And I am yet just a
Rose

Darkness

Never have I seen such darkness this night
Not even the moon or stars shared their light
It even seemed that sound was lost
On bended knees I sign the cross
For could this be the shadow of the valley of death
No odor invaded a single breath
I could sense another, I was not alone
A sensation, of feelings that I have returned home
A ghost of an echo reached my ears
Warning and pleading that I don't belong here
Then in the distance the flicker of a candle I could see
My salvation, my redemption to set myself free
From these mortal coils that we all have to face
An urging struck me, that I had to leave this place
Adeline pumping, I was ready to run or fight
As long as I could until I reached this light
With each step forward brighter became the light
But with that, such horrors filled my sight
The path I traveled was not made of stones
But that of the lost, dead and decaying bones
Each foot fall an eerie sound it would make
Snapping and cracking of bones that brake
A thought how could this be the tunnel to ever lasting peace
The light is so far away, that I'll never reach
Once again, the echo, "you can do this come back home"

A strength of another I would feed on since I was not alone

Soon after the images of the dead started to haunt my mind

A place to hide from it, is all I wanted to find

A startling thought that I would die here all alone

And a hapless soul would walk and crush my decaying bones

So, I prayed as I pushed forward towards this light

On this darkest of dark nights

What seemed like years of emotional and physical strain

My mind and body all burning with pain

I came upon the candle for what I sot

And it was all for not

I looked at this candle's soft glowing light

Defeated I closed my eyes then the room seemed to get bright

I opened my eyes I was on my back

The familiar echo said you died you had a heart attack.

Where do Dreams go to Die?

I want to know where dreams go to die?
Since I would visit what could have been.
I know dreams do not lay at rest at the bottom of a
bottle, since I have seen plenty.
Do they fly above the rainbows after the storm?
My problem is, that I cannot find my way out of
these dark clouds.
So please tell me where dreams go to die.
I only want to visit what might have been once
again.
The memories echo in my mind of what could have
been, but all my dreams died when doubt sneaked in.
Please tell me where my dreams are buried, so that
I can see one last time what could have been.

What is Poetry

Each time the pen touches paper
I leave a piece of me there.
One day part of my soul
Another part of my heart
It could be an idea, dream or goal
Wishful thinking for that pot of gold
But no matter what this pen writes
It is part of me as plain as sight
So this pen could be the death of me you may say
I think I'll live forever for I have too much to say
If all the pens should run out of ink
I will not hide or sink
I'll write my words with tears, sweat, and blood
Because I think, this clump of mud
For I have reason and rhyme
I pray for long life a blink of an eye in time
May my words live on forever
Not because my master of the language but because
I am cleaver
I'm not writing so that I may gloat
Or pump up my ego so it may float
But to show that poetry follows no rules
The ones that preach it are the fools
For poetry is everything and nothing all the same
Just write down some words and give it a name

Red

Red and all its shades
Comes to life in so many ways
Anger and Love just to name a few
All based on your point of view
Because someone in the days of old
Said this to be true, is what you were told
I say open up your mind
And the true meaning you will find
The color red
Is just red.

Puzzle

You are someone that fits into my puzzle of life. We all have a puzzle as we grow older, we gather the pieces and start putting our life into a big picture. We find pieces along the way that do not even belong to us, but we try anyway and sooner or later we realize they are not a fit.

In my picture there is only one piece left. I have it in my hand. I have made sure that it will fit, which it will, but I am afraid. I have been completing this puzzle my entire life and one piece remains. I am lucky enough to have found it. I can see the picture of my life without the piece, but it is not whole.

What comes next after that piece is put into place? Do I start another puzzle, or is it something totally different like a canvas with paints and brushes to paint the rest of my life? Could it be another puzzle that I share, working on this with my last piece, that helps me complete the rest of my life.

Could this last piece, be you?

The Storm

You are a beautiful chaos, and I an ugly normality. You and I are not like everyone else coming together in a peaceful silence. No, we crashed into each other you an ever-moving storm me an unmovable calm. The collision when we came together created the prefect storm. The type of storm that only the weak of heart run from; the wind the rain the lightening and thunder. You and I are either to crazy, stubborn or too strong to run from what we have made. We gain strength from each other as we stand against the storm holding each other. People will judge and will be jealous of what we have but they are the ones that ran from what all people can have we are the brave that have followed our hearts and love without limitations. The storm may get out of control at some point but, as long as we never lose sight we will be able to find the calm in the storm.

Heavy as a Brick

Some days I wish that my love could be lightweight, light as a feather to be carried on the wind to land wherever it may. But, I am not built that way. My love is heavy it cannot be lifted or moved by anyone or anything. When I fall I do not land gracefully as a feather in a bed of freshly picked cotton. I create a crater for all to see; hitting the ground with the subtly of a pallet of bricks slamming into the ground. I love deep and unconditionally which turns my heart into the broken bricks that slammed into the ground. I am left alone to pick up the pieces of clay and must put everything back together by myself. Once all is whole again on close inspection you can see the cracks in these bricks of my heart. I vowed to use these bricks to build a wall! Once I laid the last brick and happy with what I set out to do. I felt protected and satisfied with the choice that I made; never to love again.

You came into my life out of nowhere and took a brick off this wall as if it was light as a feather and set it aside. You continued to do this, you inspected each brick and repaired all the cracks that I was unable to fix. When all the bricks were restored you started fashioning them back into the shape of my heart. Now as heavy as my love is; you hold it easily with one hand, and for the first time in my life I am not afraid of the fall. I trust you with my heart and my love.

See the Unseen

Beauty is all around for us to see. A sunset or sunrise, a priceless painting, and that of a beautiful person. All these things can be and are beautiful. I feel the most beautiful things in the world are those things that you cannot see.

You see a child playing. You see the expression on their face of being happy, but that of a child's innocence, and honesty that cannot be seen is the true beauty.

A couple smiling and walking down the street hand in hand you can see that they are in love by the way they act towards each other. The unseen caring, tenderness they share is the priceless beauty.

A new mother and father seeing their child for the first time. The pride, as well as the humbling feelings, all the hopes and dreams these new parents have for their child. That is pure beauty.

All that I try to write about all these beautiful unseen things that you feel, letting your heart be filled with warmth. Even though my words can never do justice on behalf of these feelings, until you see the unseen.

Acknowledgements

Where to start? My Fans. If you are reading this then you are a Fan, or a Critic, and I want to take this time to thank you for taking the time for reading and experiencing the journey that I hope I was able to give to you. Thank you to my Critics either you loved it or hated it. I welcome all the feedback.

My Family! I know that I can be a pain, with all the different ideas, after ideas. I am the dreamer of the family and there is no dream too big. So, my dear Sister, thank you for being my tether to the world of reality. You are my rock, that keeps me grounded. I know that you will never read this book, well I hope that none of my family reads this book it would be too awkward for how I wrote it.

My Friends! You are the ones that let me dream and causes my Sister all the headaches. I would have never done this without your help and support. I do understand the awkward feeling that you have towards me now after some of you have read rough draft after rough draft. But, truly thank you.

To a special young lady. The first to read a few pages and asked for more. I do not know how or what you did but when you asked, "Have you ever thought about having this published?" Was it the subtle encouragement, the simple question that I never really asked myself, or something else? I ask myself these questions daily as I continue to write. I owe you more than I can ever repay, mere words of Thanks could ever convey.

To anyone else that may feel that they deserve a thanks or pat on the back that I forgot to mention. This is the first book that I have ever written, so please keep that in mind.

Thank you everyone and I do hope that you enjoyed and had a wonderful experience reading this.